MURDER to my EARS

an octavia fields mystery

REBECCA MCKINNON

ISBN: 9798988278207

One

"NOT THIS ONE. I NEED the twenty-five gauge E string with the ball. This is a twenty-six gauge with a loop." Ludwig flicked the little string envelope away from himself with more force than the situation called for.

My glasses were slipping down my nose, but even with the vintage cat-eye frames blocking part of my vision I could see the envelope smack Mairi in the middle of her heart-shaped face.

"This is the only gauge we carry in this brand." Mairi's voice was tight.

I should probably step in, but Mairi hated it when I tried to fix problems, even though it was my shop. The look on her face made me think she wished I was five miles away instead of five feet. Maybe if I acted like I wasn't listening it would be enough. I flexed my bare toes against the cool tiles and reached into the box on top of the glass display case and pulled out more rosin.

"One of these boxes must have the right string,"

Ludwig said in that insufferable tone mastered by every snooty musician.

I'm not saying every musician is snooty. That would be telling tales about myself and some of my best friends. But some musicians had more ego than talent.

Ludwig had talent. A lot of it. So when I tell you his ego was twice as big as his talent, well, it's saying something.

"I'm sorry, sir, it's not on the inventory list. If you want to try a different brand I could give you a twenty-five. I could probably talk my boss into giving you a discount for your understanding." Mairi glanced my way, so I pretended I wasn't watching.

The day I gave Ludwig Baylor a discount would be the day I closed up shop for good.

Okay, so maybe you noticed Ludwig's not my favorite person. Once upon a time we'd been friendly. That was before it was glaringly clear that he valued his perfect pitch more than any of the people in his life.

"How can you not have this in a twenty-five?" Ludwig's voice was getting louder. "Everyone knows this is what I use."

The frustrated vibes pouring off Mairi were seriously messing with my setting-up-shop-for-the-season high.

"Octavia, tell her." Ludwig turned to me, completely ruining any chance that I could stay out of things.

I pushed the glasses up right before they slid off the tip of my nose. "The only reason anyone knows what strings you use is because you insist on yelling about it. We don't have the strings because you never shop here, Ludwig. You make a big deal about not shopping here."

He muttered something under his breath. I only managed to catch the word "hippie," but I didn't need the look on his face to tell me it wasn't complimentary.

Like I said, we had history. And not the romantic kind.

I abandoned the rosin and finally gave him my full attention. "What happened to getting a better deal online?"

He tapped his finger on the counter. The sound set my jaw on edge.

The counter was actually the top of a glass display case. See, my violin shop used to be a gift shop, and I kept the octagon of glass display cases. One edge was missing so staff could go *behind the counter.*

The display fit the room. Literally. The room was octagonal, and the front half of it was windows. I think it had been a gazebo in a former life. Then a rectangle had been built coming off the back half of it. One room off the back of the shop was an office. Another was an instrument and practice room. The biggest room was a workshop for the luthiers a friend of mine loaned me from his shop each summer.

What? It's not like I know how to do sound post adjustments or glue seams. It benefited everyone. My shop was where the musicians were. Really. Aerie Pines was the summer home of the Aerie Peaks Symphony.

Not only that, but down the road one way there was a summer music program for college students—not exactly like a summer camp, but calling it one means you'll have a good idea what it's like.

If you take the road in the other direction there's a summer music camp for high schoolers, sponsored by a different college than the other one.

So, see, it was lucrative for my shop and for the luthiers.

Some of the musicians were fun to have around. Others—well, others were like Ludwig.

Insufferable.

"My order didn't arrive before coming to this compound." His mouth twisted with distaste. "I've asked Cora to bring it up to me once it arrives, but until then, I need a string."

"Well, you can buy what we have or not, but I can't make a string appear out of thin air." I paused. Calling Aerie Pines a compound wasn't nice—mainly because I knew what Ludwig's definition of a compound was. But that wasn't what really irked me. "Did you really ask your ex-wife to drive two hours each way just to bring you a string?"

Ludwig looked at me like I was a bug he wanted to squash.

Just try it, I thought.

"What I do or do not do is none of your business."

Somebody was touchy.

The big glass doors swung open dramatically behind Ludwig. A short woman with curves in all the right places paused dramatically before practically dancing forward.

Piper's grand entrance made me grin. We hadn't seen each other in two months—and I'd missed my best friend. She tilted her chestnut brown modernized Marilyn Monroe hair toward Ludwig with a roll of her eyes.

I tried not to laugh as I turned back to my customer. If that's what he was. "Are you going to buy something or not?"

His derisive glance took in Piper, and Mairi, and me. "This was a waste of time."

"Don't let the door hit you on the way out," Piper chirped.

Ludwig's nose tipped a few degrees higher in the air as he spun on his heel.

Piper didn't wait for him to disappear before she started digging into the boxes of stock. "Is this that new kind of instrument polish, Octavia? Where do you want it?"

I looked around the display cases. "Wherever you want."

Mairi clapped her hand over her generous mouth as a whimper escaped.

She wasn't a fan of the way I organized the stock.

"Mairi and Xavier will rearrange everything

after I leave." I bit the inside of my cheek to hold back a smile.

Mairi frowned, her cheeks pink.

"Maybe if we put them in good places to start with," Piper suggested drily, "your staff wouldn't have to rearrange everything and trust you didn't remember where you'd put things in the first place."

Whatever. Rearranging things gave the two of them something to do when I wasn't there, and they enjoyed watching me search for things that had moved since I'd put them down.

I usually claimed things had sprouted feet, and we all pretended like I didn't know they were the ones who really ran the shop.

Piper was looking toward the closed doors at the back of the shop. "Where is Xavier, anyway?"

Mairi cleared her throat. "Setting up the office."

Piper's shoulders heaved with a sigh. "Oh."

"He has to be almost done. He's been in there for ages," I said, even though I had no idea how long he'd been working on it. "Don't worry, you'll get to enjoy the eye candy soon."

"Shh! He might hear you." Piper gave me a look I recognized. It was one she wore a lot, at least around me.

I shrugged. Xavier wouldn't mind the label—he'd enjoy knowing Piper liked looking at him. He had the whole dark, smoldering thing going for him. Dark and smoldering had been Piper's weakness since she and I met when we were assigned to the same dorm room in college.

That's right, I went to college. Well, a music conservatory.

I lasted a whole month before realizing all the music theory and solfeggio just distracted from everything I loved about playing the viola.

When they very bluntly told me I was keeping the other students from learning, I handed in my dorm key and left. But the friendship between Piper and me stuck, which meant I'd met the whole parade of dark and smoldering that had marched through Piper's life. She never met most of them, except through the magic of television and movies.

Xavier chose that moment to sashay out of the office, opening the door in a flurry and making an entrance that almost rivaled Piper's. "Is that awful man gone?"

"For now." Mairi waved her hands toward where Piper and I were looking for somewhere to put the instrument polish. "Octavia put the rosin next to the shoulder rests."

Xavier's dark eyes widened. He dropped the lock of shoulder-length hair he'd been twirling around a long finger and hurried over, either ignoring or not noticing the way Piper looked at him. "No, no, no. The rosin should be with the polishing cloths and instrument polish. Rosin makes the dust, the cloths clean it up, and you use the cloths for the polish. It all goes together."

I crossed my arms. "Do you want to set up the shop so I don't make any other drastic mistakes?"

He nodded as if it was the first thing that had gone right all day. "Yes. Yes, that's a good idea. You could help Piper move into her summer apartment. Or take a walk around the lake. Or go home and make sure you're set up for the summer."

I stepped back, my hands up as if I was about to be arrested. "Chill out, I was joking. Of course I'm going to help set things up here."

Piper sighed as she stared dreamily at Xavier.

I snapped my fingers in front of her face until she came out of it. "Does your husband know you're here?"

Startled by the reminder she was staring, she turned away from Xavier.

I should probably tell you Piper was madly in love with her husband, a bassoonist in the symphony. Luckily, he was smart enough to insist he didn't care who she looked at, as long as she came home to him.

Even if Piper hadn't been married, nothing would have happened between her and Xavier.

Xavier was in a committed relationship with himself.

Yes, you heard that right.

Xavier was convinced relationships with other people were too much pressure—and judging by the two significant others he'd had in the time I'd known him, he had a point—so he decided to be alone.

"Of course my husband knows I'm here. He told

me to run off to visit you while he unpacked." Piper gave me a triumphant grin. "He's trying to make sure he gets the bigger closet."

"You don't want it?"

"Oh, Octavia. Letting him think he's winning by getting the bigger closet means he's going to give me anything else I want when I get home." Her eyes sparkled. "I'm going to get the second bedroom as my music studio, which means I won't have to sign up for one of the practice cabins."

I smiled. "The practice cabins are fun."

They were. They had more space than any musician needed, and were furnished with comfortable couches. And every year there were at least a couple musicians whose cabins saw as many trysts as practice sessions.

Piper took in my smile, and her eyes widened. "I want to talk about this. Later."

"Ladies." Xavier's voice jolted me back to the shop. "Go. Do things. Let us take care of the shop."

"They never give up, do they?" Piper asked.

I shook my head.

"You could go find Mr. Baylor and tell him not to come back," Mairi suggested.

"What was he upset about this time?" Xavier asked.

"We didn't have the string he wanted." Mairi rolled her eyes and started pulling out all the stock I'd tried to organize.

They weren't even going to wait for me to leave this year.

I tried to be offended, but I didn't really want to embrace those negative vibes.

Piper whistled. "Ludwig's in high dudgeon today."

Xavier leaned across the display case until he was as close to Piper as he could get. "What's he done?"

It took Piper half a dozen breaths and at least a hundred eyelash flutters to get herself under control.

She doted on her husband, really she did, but she could never seem to keep herself from flirting with anyone dark and smoldering.

"Ludwig went into a rampage at rehearsal this morning." Her eyelashes fluttered again, but whatever juicy gossip was involved meant Piper was as oblivious to those eyelashes as Xavier was. "It's all anyone can talk about."

"Do tell." From Xavier, this was practically begging.

Mairi stopped undoing all my work and crossed the few steps to join us.

"Rehearsal was a disaster. The first one after we move up here for the summer always is. Everyone's caught up in the move, but that brings a lot of excitement, too. Some of the musicians were goofing off, which is basically an unspoken tradition at this point."

I remembered that from my season with them. That's right, I made it a whole season before realizing playing with the symphony wasn't for me.

But really, you can only take getting told off for being late or missing rehearsal so many times. I decided to find a job where time wasn't so important. Since this shop is only a summer gig, and since Mairi and Xavier were really the ones running it, I'd made it work for three years now.

Okay, this would be the third, but who's counting?

"The next rehearsal should be a little easier," I offered. I reached into a box and started pulling out mutes. I could at least unpack boxes while we talked, even if my ever-so-capable staff wouldn't let me organize things.

"Who cares if rehearsals are easy? Get to the juicy part of the story." Xavier trailed a finger in a long, winding path across the glass in front of him.

Piper's eyes took on a dreamy quality as she watched his finger. As soon as it stilled, she shook her head and started talking again. "Ludwig stopped the conductor and yelled at us. None of us are worthy of his excellent leadership, or of performing on his stage, or breathing his air, yada, yada, yada. If we don't turn things around, he's going to get each and every person fired."

"Can he do that?" Mairi asked. "I thought there were contracts and a union."

"He can't, but he likes to think being concertmaster gives him more leverage than the other musicians." I said, catching my glasses on the tip of my finger and pushing them back up the bridge of my nose. I'd hate to see what Ludwig would do with any real power. "I don't know how you put up with him as your stand partner."

"You get used to him." Piper paused as she thought. "I mostly just ignore him. Anyway, rehearsal ended early after his hissy fit, and everyone's either laughing or grumbling behind his back."

At the back of the store, the door leading into the instrument workshop opened. Xavier's hips started to sway to the Latin beat that spilled out.

Eli, one of the luthiers I'd borrowed for the summer, paused in the doorway. He was so tall his salt and pepper hair brushed against the lintel. "Octavia, didn't you need that bow?"

Eli specialized in bow repairs, and it was a good thing he did. You'd be surprised how quickly a musician needed a rehair when they played so many hours a day. Or when they just liked to break hairs during a performance because they were too aggressive. Besides, it looked groovy to have those loose bow hairs floating around the performer's head.

Okay, fine. Sometimes hairs just break, and it's not because people played too hard, or wanted to look groovy. Unless you're a string musician yourself, you'll just have to take my word for it.

"Octavia?" he prompted.

"What?"

"The bow. The one that lost the plug and needed to be rehaired. Didn't you need that at noon?"

Now, you might be thinking Eli was starting to

sound annoyed, but you'd be wrong. He was laughing. Somehow all the people who worked for me were easily amused by me.

Go figure.

"Oh, right." I finally remembered the bow he was talking about. "I'm supposed to meet Tatiana at the amphitheater with it at noon."

"It's a quarter past."

Impossible.

My stomach grumbled that he was right.

"You'd better hurry," Piper piped in. "You never know what kind of a mood Tatiana's going to be in."

Two

I KNOW WHAT YOU'RE THINKING, but Tatiana wasn't like Ludwig.

Sure, she could be temperamental, but she's an *artiste*. *Artistes* are allowed to be temperamental. And while the second violin principal was a diva, she could absolutely be nice.

To other people.

But she and I had gotten off on the wrong foot when she tried to steal my boyfriend—are they still boyfriends when you're in your thirties? Manfriend didn't sound right, and significant other sounded *too* significant, if you know what I mean—and he said thanks, but he preferred me.

And could she ever hold a grudge.

Morton and I weren't even together anymore.

That was still kinda new. He—

You know what? I don't want to talk about it. I don't know you well enough yet.

My point is, Tatiana King would remember I was late for the rest of her life.

I held on tight to that bow case as I took the path outside my shop past the small lake, the benches, the brass and woodwind shop, and the auditorium.

After going down a tier—Aerie Pines was on the side of the mountain, of course there were tiers—I passed all the offices, waving briefly at a couple staff members enjoying their lunch in the sunshine.

Instead of following the paths, I hurried across the giant lawn toward the amphitheater, not even taking time to squidge my toes in the grass. Because I was really late by that time, that's why.

The musician's door took far too long to come into view, but eventually I got there. I reached for the handle and yanked.

The door rattled but didn't open.

I tried again.

Why was it locked? Tatiana wouldn't have left. She'd be pacing around somewhere in there waiting for me, but we'd known each other long enough for her to know I sometimes lost track of time.

Okay, my internal clock moved at a very different speed than normal clocks, but still.

The only reason she would have left was to come to the shop to pick up the bow herself, and I hadn't passed her on my way here.

I knocked on the door and waited.

And waited.

"Tatiana!" I knocked again, harder this time. Where was she?

I walked around the back of the amphitheater to

the tall garage doors used for stage equipment and some of the larger instruments. As expected, they were closed, but if I was lucky the small door beside them would be unlocked.

Turned out I wasn't lucky.

I continued to circle the amphitheater, failing to find any unlocked doors.

Loitering outside the musician's door, I went over my options. There weren't as many as you might think. I could take the bow back to my shop and wait for her to show up. Or, since it was possible Tatiana was sitting in the greenroom and hadn't heard me knock, I could find someone on the security staff to let me in.

I made my way to the looped path between the amphitheater and the parking lot and followed it to the security office.

The deck was empty but the door was propped open, so I let myself inside without knocking. Every head in the room turned, and suddenly a dozen eyes were on me.

Of course, I'd stepped right into the middle of a security team meeting.

"Everything okay, Octavia?"

I blinked at Hector.

His eyes crinkled as he grinned. "I'm not sure you've ever stepped through that door."

If anyone had asked me, I'd have said Hector was too good-natured to be head of security anywhere, even at some trendy little strip mall. The man was always happy.

If anyone had asked Piper, she'd have said he was too young and good-looking to be head of security, and that he should be modeling underwear on billboards.

Yes, I'm sure that's what she'd say. Because we'd talked about it one night last summer, okay?

"I'm supposed to be delivering a bow to the amphitheater for one of the violinists." I jiggled the bow case in my hand as evidence. "The door is locked, and the greenroom is far enough away from the door that she didn't hear me knocking. Can someone let me in?"

Hector's gaze traveled across his team. "Everyone clear on your assignments? Good, then we're done here. I'll be over at the amphitheater with Octavia if anyone needs me."

As the rest of the team went about their business, Hector led me to the door. "One of these days I'll convince the board to put in modern doorknobs where everyone can have their own code to get in. Save people from having this problem."

I stepped back out into the sunshine. "I didn't take you as the kind of guy to want to police all the comings and goings."

"It's not about policing people, or even knowing where people are. It's about making sure people have access to the places they should."

Yeah, sure. It wouldn't surprise me to find out the board had approved security cameras for the entire mountainside. Under the guise of protecting us, of course.

"It wouldn't have helped today," I said. Since there were shrubs and other large plants in the area between the four buildings on this loop and the amphitheater, we followed the path instead of cutting across. "I'm not with the symphony, so I'm not really supposed to be backstage unless I'm invited."

Hector had the kind of laugh that drew attention. When it spilled out of him, an administrator who was walking past stared so intently she almost lost her balance. Since she would have paid for that with a sprained ankle—really, who in their right mind wore heels in the mountains?—it was good she spun back around before falling on her face.

The walkie-talkie thing on Hector's hip let out a squawk, and he adjusted the volume. "I have the feeling nothing much keeps you from going wherever you want."

I made a noncommittal sound, and he laughed again.

When we reached the musician's door, he pulled out his keys. He opened the door and motioned me inside, then followed.

"I need a babysitter?" I teased. I didn't mind having him along. There were expensive instruments back here—I mean, it's not like the percussionists or the harpist were about to haul their instruments up to the apartments, was it?—

and it was good to know Hector was serious about keeping them safe.

We passed a clock, and I frowned. How did it get to be one o'clock? "She's really going to hate me for being late."

"She'll have to understand," Hector said. "It's not your fault the door was locked."

Ha! This was only his second summer here—well, he was only twenty-three or twenty-four, of course he hadn't been here long—so he didn't quite get how diva-y some of these musicians could be.

No, not all of them. Didn't I already say that?

The doors to the greenroom stood open, but the lights were off.

I paused on the threshold. "Tatiana?"

Nothing.

I looked at Hector. "Maybe she left."

Hector stepped inside, reaching over to flick the light on.

One wall of the greenroom was lined with cubbies for the musicians to put their cases. Another held doors I knew led to dressing rooms. The main part of the room was filled with collections of furniture where musicians could gather to relax and visit during breaks and before performances.

After being closed up for so many months, an odd mustiness lingered in the air. I wrinkled my nose against the scent and tried not to breathe too deeply.

"Maybe she's in a dressing room," I offered. As I started toward the doors, I noticed a violin case on one of the couches. It was an expensive one, with all the bells and whistles.

I changed course, winding through the furniture, heading for the case to see if it was Tatiana's. If I couldn't find her, I could at least put her bow in the case so it would be there when she needed it.

Rounding a particularly large couch, I caught sight of a shoe.

My stomach dropped. The shoe was attached to a leg, as so many of them are.

Had Tatiana had an accident? I shook myself. That was silly—it wasn't a woman's shoe.

I moved a bit more. The legs were attached to a torso, and arms, and a head.

"Hector?" My voice shook. "I need you."

The security guard came forward. "What is it?"

I gestured to the violinist sprawled on the floor.

Hector moved forward cautiously. He crouched down, reaching for the man's neck. As he felt for a pulse, the man's head wobbled and I caught sight of the familiar face.

Oh, no. I swallowed hard. "Is he—?"

Hector glanced up at me, as if waiting, but I couldn't finish the question.

He couldn't be dead. I just talked to him.

"He's gone." Hector snapped his fingers to get my attention. "You should back up so you don't contaminate the crime scene."

"Crime scene?" I stammered.

Yes, I know. You think because I try to roll with things, a dead body shouldn't phase me.

You try finding a body and see how you handle it.

Hector nodded. Behind the kindness in his eyes was something hard and determined, but what made it all come crashing down on me was the fact that he wasn't smiling.

And like I mentioned, Hector was always smiling.

"Do you know him?" Hector asked.

I nodded. Of course I did. "That's Ludwig Baylor. The concertmaster."

Three

ON HECTOR'S ORDERS, I STOOD outside the musician's door, ready to deter anyone who might decide to take advantage of the greenroom being unscheduled.

Not that any of the musicians could get in without a key, but there was always a chance someone besides me might think of getting security to let them through the locked door.

My secondary job was to let in the cops when they got here. I had Hector's nice, shiny key in my pocket in case they got here before he came back from securing the outside of the amphitheater. He didn't want anyone sneaking in—or out. Because apparently someone might have still been there when we walked in, and if they were hiding they weren't going to escape on his watch.

I dug my big toe into the dirt path, watching the glitter in my nail polish sparkle in the sunlight.

Birds chirped as a breeze escaped the nearby trees.

Sunshine, and birds, and the scent of evergreens.

It seemed wrong, somehow, for the world to be so peaceful when someone had just died, even when it was a miserable creature like Ludwig.

On the other hand, I didn't know anyone who would celebrate the man's life, or his self-centered energy. Oh, they might pretend to, but on the inside they'd be ambivalent.

Finally, Hector made his way back to me. "Anything to report?"

As if I were on his team. I chuckled, then grimaced. "No one's come close."

"Good. Sorry I had to ask for your help. My guys will be here as soon as they can."

I looked toward the parking lot, hopeful. "So I can go?"

Hector's smile was back, but it was faint, and full of apology. "You're the one who found the body. The police are going to need to talk to you."

Ugh. Of course they were.

Somehow, Hector straightened, despite his already perfect posture. "And here they come."

I looked down the path again.

The three people walking toward us were over-dressed. Instead of wearing shorts or something else appropriate to summer in the mountains, they were in suits. Even if they hadn't been, their movements would have given them away. They walked like cops, their long strides as sure as if they owned the place.

For all I knew, they did. I mean, who actually

owned Aerie Pines? I had no idea. Unless maybe the symphony owned it? But really, if they couldn't afford to give the musicians better salaries, could they really have a budget to pay for all this? Unless they'd spent all their money on the land instead of the musicians.

As the trio in suits got closer, I could make out a little more about them.

The man on the end had a medium build and dark hair. His suit was a little rumpled.

On the other end was a petite woman who somehow managed to walk straight while swinging her head around, taking in everything in the area.

In the middle was the man who was obviously in charge. He was larger than the others, especially through the shoulders. His suit was impeccable, and his short sandy hair ruffled in the breeze. His eyes were hidden behind sunglasses, but I could feel the weight of his stare.

Suddenly, my linen shorts paired with the patchwork peasant top felt shabby and inappropriate. I'd chosen them to match the excitement I'd felt about setting up the shop, not for being stared at by some guy in a suit. I squared my shoulders.

It wasn't as if I'd started out the day with any idea Aerie Pines would host a death.

Or that I'd be the one to find the body.

Or that it would be someone I knew and disliked.

That was the problem, wasn't it? I didn't like

him, and we'd had words just a little while before he died.

Hector stepped forward as they came to a stop. "Detectives, thanks for coming. I'm in charge of security here. Hector Murillo."

"You're the one who called in?" The man removed the sunglasses and tucked them into his pocket. His sharp blue eyes didn't leave Hector's face, but I knew he was registering every twitch of my hands.

I grabbed my hair and tossed it over my shoulder.

"I am." Hector motioned to the door. "It's just through here."

"Your team has secured the area?" The detective reached for the door. It rattled.

Hector glanced at me.

I scooped the key out of my pocket and handed it to him.

The detective's gaze landed on me, stronger without the shield of his sunglasses.

A shiver started at the base of my spine. Not wanting the detective to think he'd gotten the best of me, I splayed my toes and forced the energy into the ground instead of up my back.

Hector cleared his throat. "They'll be here shortly. Aerie Pines is just opening for the season today, so they've been busy elsewhere. I secured everything."

"And the key?"

"Ah." One of Hector's famous smiles flitted

briefly across his face. "Octavia is the one who found the body. I asked her to keep the key in case you arrived before I finished."

The detective shot a glance at his companions. I didn't exactly know what it meant, but based on the way everyone stared at me, it wasn't too hard to come up with a ballpark idea.

The woman gave a small nod.

Hector unlocked the door and held it open.

The head detective ducked inside while the other two approached me.

The woman offered a sympathetic smile. "You found the body?"

I nodded. "Hector was with me."

"I'm going to need you to tell me about it. Do you need to sit down? Have some water?"

I shook my head. "I'd rather just get it over with."

The man chuckled. "I'm afraid it won't be fast. By the time we're done here, you'll never want to talk about it again."

I already never wanted to talk about it, so that wasn't saying much.

"I'm Detective Locke," he said. He held out a hand.

Shaking his hand was . . . weird. I could only assume he was trying to manipulate me by being polite. "Octavia Fields."

"I'm Detective Watson." The woman didn't offer her hand.

"Watson?" I asked. I thought Watson was a doctor, not a detective.

Come on, I know you had the same reaction.

Detective Locke shouldn't play poker. He couldn't disguise his laughing eyes, or the tightness around his lips as he held in his amusement. "You know Sir Arthur Conan Doyle."

"Everyone knows Sherlock and Watson." How could anyone avoid knowing them? Even if a person didn't like to read, the number of tv shows and movies about the duo kept them relevant.

"Wait until you hear her first name." Detective Locke bit his lip.

"Is this really the time?" Detective Watson sighed. "We're supposed to be taking her statement."

"It's Irene," he whispered.

"Ms. Fields. Can I call you Octavia?" Detective Watson asked.

Knowing what could happen if I got on the wrong side of a cop, I shared a quick smile with Detective Locke, then gave my attention to Detective Watson. Irene. "Of course."

"Please tell me what happened."

As I recounted the reason I'd been there, and why I'd made sure Hector had come along—the woman's suspicion about that was a good reminder that these two weren't my friends, no matter how at ease they tried to make me—the two of them tapped notes into their phones.

As I finished, the rest of their team arrived.

Detective Locke tucked his phone back in his

pocket. "Thanks, Octavia. Go ahead and take a seat over there until Detective Price is ready for you."

"But I already told you everything." I mean, I know they had to investigate the death, but I had other things to do.

Yes, I know Mairi and Xavier could set up the shop without me, but I really should be there to oversee it all.

"Detective Price always talks to the first on the scene," Detective Watson said. "It's procedure."

They turned away.

I made my way over to the benches facing the stage. Ludwig had been a pain in my neck when he was alive, and somehow he didn't see fit to change now that he was dead.

I sat sideways on the wooden bench, leaning back on my hands with my legs stretched out along the boards and watched as Hector's team finally arrived.

The place was crawling with more security than an unlawful demonstration at a protest.

Someone had blocked off the amphitheater with police tape, but it was pulled aside for one of the park's golf carts to get through.

A stretcher was strapped to the back of it.

My stomach twisted at the sight.

Ludwig was really dead.

Hector had called it a crime scene and hustled me out of there as fast as he could while he called for the detectives, but every time I closed my eyes I could see Ludwig's slack face.

"Ms. Fields?"

I tore my eyes away from the people scurrying in and out and looked around. There, on the stage, was the broad shouldered detective with the piercing blue eyes.

Eyes that were trained on me as if he was trying to decide something important, like if I was his main suspect.

I stood up and made my way to the edge of the stage as he descended the narrow, unobtrusive stairs where the stage met the wall at the back of what would normally be the violin section.

"I'm ready for you now. Mr. Murillo's agreed to let me use the security office." Without really looking at me, he started walking away.

Who was Mr. Murillo?

I caught sight of Hector through the stage door, and things clicked into place.

Look, I was kind of distracted by the whole finding a body thing. You can't really expect me to be thinking straight.

Suddenly, the detective was at my side, his hand on my elbow. "Come with me."

What? But I didn't do anything. "Are you kidding me? I have things to do—I don't have time to get arrested today. Maybe you should come back tomorrow."

He paused, and those blue eyes bored into mine. "You seem to be more concerned about the timing than the idea of being arrested."

"It wouldn't be the first time I've been tossed

into the back of a police cruiser."

He widened his stance. "What were you arrested for?"

This was getting awkward. "Which time?"

"You've been arrested more than once?"

Did I imagine that growl in his voice? "Yes."

He worked his jaw. "Twice?"

Yes. Definitely awkward. "Um, more than that."

I know what you're wondering, because I was wondering it, too. Why hadn't he pulled out the handcuffs yet?

He hooked the thumb of his free hand at his hip.

I glanced at his belt to see if he was getting ready to grab his cuffs.

"How many times have you been arrested, Octavia Fields?"

His voice sent a trickle of anticipation down my spine. My eyes jumped back to his face. "Do people actually keep track of that?"

It was as if he didn't think people had better things to worry about.

Things moved pretty quickly after that.

Detective What's-His-Bucket used his grip on my elbow to guide me to Hector's office.

He was oddly gentle about it. More like he was propelling me instead of dragging me.

Yeah, I know, it didn't make sense to me, either.

As we walked, I couldn't help but notice the people gathering on the other side of the police tape.

Of course word had gotten out. That police tape is designed to stand out. Throw in all the extra people who weren't expected to show up and the gossips were out in force.

Except Xavier. He must have taken his job of organizing my shop seriously.

"Octavia?" Piper's voice drifted across to me.

I waved at her with the bow case in my uncaptured hand.

Well, I guess that meant the gossips were all covered, because there was no way Piper wouldn't race back to the shop to tell Xavier.

"Friend of yours?" the detective asked.

"Yep."

"Maybe *she* knows how many times you've been arrested," he muttered.

The comment wasn't really meant for me—he'd have spoken louder if it was—but I couldn't stop myself from replying. "Probably not. She doesn't really like numbers."

As soon as the growing crowd disappeared behind the shrubs, his hold loosened.

It felt wrong. I couldn't decide if it was because I expected his hold to tighten, or if it was something else.

I fumbled for a way to break the strange tension around us. Maybe something to say.

He didn't look like he'd appreciate being told his pristine suit was speckled with bright yellow pollen. His shoulders looked like the sunlight had decided to kiss him.

It probably wasn't the time to ask if he saw Watson and Locke as sidekicks, or if they were an actual team. How did that work? I mean, he was in charge, right? But they were all detectives.

Maybe I should ask how far they had to come? The ranger station wouldn't have kept detectives in a cabin just in case they were ever needed.

"You haven't read me my rights." I winced. Any of my other thoughts would have been better than reminding him he was in the middle of arresting me.

Although I did wish he'd just get on with it so my attorney could start working on getting me released.

Detective Stone-Face didn't say anything, just helped me up the two steps and across the deck to the security office.

As soon as I stepped through the door, he released my elbow.

I looked around the room. When I'd come in before, the room had felt crowded with people. Now I realized it wasn't as small as it had seemed.

The detective disappeared through a door, only to reappear a few seconds later with two bottles of water. "Have a seat."

The room didn't have any desks, but it did have a table with half a dozen chairs in the middle of the room. "Where?"

I didn't love the idea of sitting directly across from him. It would feel too much like I was in one of those boxy little rooms they take you to interrogate you.

Yes, of course I've been in those before. That doesn't mean I like them.

"Anywhere you'd like."

I pulled out the chair on one end of the table and sat down.

The detective sat in the chair next to me and set one of the bottles of water in front of me. "You must be thirsty after your shock."

The bottle was already forming little beads of condensation on the outside.

My mouth watered, and I reached for it.

Look, I'm not stupid. I know they do that trick where they get you to touch something just so they can get your fingerprints. But face it, my prints were already in the system. This guy would have no problem getting them if he wanted to, and quite frankly, my belly was empty.

I'd missed lunch for this mess.

I twisted off the cap and took a swig, surprised when the detective did the same.

He set his bottle on the table and fished his phone out of his pocket. After reading something, he set it down and looked at me. He had the kind of eyes that felt like they were seeing past the surface. "You knew the victim?"

"Everyone around here knows Ludwig. He's the concertmaster." I ran my finger through some of the condensation beads, trying not to meet his eyes. They made me feel like I should be remembering every little thing I'd done wrong so they could be explained away.

"What does that mean?"

"Look, Detective —?"

"Price."

"Detective Price." Huh. After meeting Detective Watson, somehow I'd expected a name that felt more . . . detective-y for the lead detective.

I mean, it's not like everyone could be named after Sherlock characters, right? But there are a lot of other detectives out there.

Poirot? Marple?

No, Detective Price wouldn't make a good Miss Marple. He couldn't have been much older than me, for a start. Thirty-five doesn't feel old enough for Miss Marple.

And, of course, I don't imagine Miss Marple ever looked like *that*.

"Ms. Fields?"

"The concertmaster is a leader. It's always the first chair in the first violins." There was a lot more to it than that, but it was hard to put into words. I searched for a different way to put it. "Sometimes you get a conductor who doesn't know what they're doing, and the musicians follow the concertmaster instead of the conductor. Without saying anything, of course."

"So they're important."

I nodded and pushed my glasses back up my nose. Piper kept telling me I should take them in and get them adjusted, but I was afraid they'd ruin the frame.

What? They're vintage.

Detective Price's eyes took on a shrewd glint. "I'm not familiar with the classical music world, so maybe you can help me with what happens now. Is the symphony leaderless?"

"No. The associate concertmaster will take over. And the different sections all have principals, too, to lead their group. They set the bowings, and play the solo parts, and that kind of thing." Eventually they'd put out a notice for open auditions for a new concertmaster, but my guess was the board would hold off on that for a little while.

"So this associate concertmaster is looking at a promotion." He reached for his water bottle and unscrewed the top. "That sounds like a pretty good motive."

Uh-oh.

Four

"PIPER COULDN'T HAVE KILLED HIM."

Don't look at me that way. I hadn't meant to throw my best friend under the bus.

Detective Jump-To-Conclusions took a sip of water before answering. "This violinist's name is Piper?"

"Yes. But she didn't kill him. Ludwig was still in my shop when she came in, and she hadn't left when I headed down to the amphitheater to take this bow to Tatiana."

"The victim was in your shop?" He picked the phone up again and started scrolling through something. Probably the notes from my little chat with the other detectives. "What was he doing there?"

My mouth was faster than my brain. "Causing problems, as usual."

Detective Price stared until I started talking again.

"You're going to find out sooner or later." I took

a deep breath. If I was lucky, karma wouldn't hate me for telling the truth. "Ludwig wasn't a very nice guy."

"Tell me about it," he ordered.

So I did.

I tried to stick to the facts, explaining how he belittled Mairi, and was caught up in his own greatness to the point that no one else mattered.

"I wonder, what would the victim have told me about you?"

Ha! That was so easy I didn't even have to think. I tilted my head and smiled. "That I'm a hippie who's so bad at life no one wants to be around me."

Finally, something caught Detective I'm-In-Charge off guard. He blinked. "Excuse me?"

"That's what he'd say if you could ask him about me."

"That no one wants to be around you." He paused, then shook his head. "What gives you that idea?"

I shrugged. "One nice thing I can say about Ludwig is that he'd never bother saying anything behind your back that he wouldn't say to your face."

Something about this bothered the detective, but I couldn't tell what.

And then I realized something. I know, I should have thought of it before, but cops don't usually want to *talk* to me. They just want to haul me in and put me in a holding cell until my lawyer worked things out.

This whole thing with Detective Let's-Have-A-Conversation threw me.

I reached out and grabbed his wrist. "Hold up. Why are you having me explain why Piper couldn't have killed Ludwig if you're arresting me for it?"

He stared at my hand.

The heat of his skin seeped into my fingertips.

Oops. I hadn't meant to actually touch him. I let go, rubbing my fingers against my shorts for good measure, but my fingers still tingled.

"I never said I was arresting you."

Just because he didn't say I was under arrest didn't mean he hadn't planned to arrest me as soon as I told him anything interesting.

He cocked his head as if I was something unusual he needed to study to understand. "You were serious about reading your rights before? I assure you, I always inform suspects when I place them under arrest."

Huh. Maybe he wasn't trying to trick me.

I wasn't sure how to react to that.

"I'll want to speak with Piper to confirm she was where you say. If that checks out I can cross her off my suspect list." He glanced toward the door. "Could you send her a text to meet you here, without telling her why?"

"Nope. I don't have a phone."

He leaned toward me, as if getting closer would help my words make sense. "You don't have a phone."

I don't know why everyone always gets hung up

on that. People act like they can't live without a phone.

Sorry, bad choice of words.

But you know what I mean. It blows my mind that people want to keep a cancer-causing, anxiety-inducing, constantly-interrupting, always-*there* tracking device in their pocket.

Life was much more zen without the distraction.

Detective Doesn't-Understand cleared his throat. "Okay. I can have my team track her down."

"You could do that."

He smiled.

I swear the world stopped spinning for two seconds.

You know how in romance books the author says the hero's smile was devastating? I'd never gotten that. A smile is a smile. A glimpse of the inner person whose face was wearing it.

When Detective Devastating smiled, I wanted him to toss me in jail just so I'd have an excuse to see him a little longer. His eyes were more intense, with a wicked edge to his gaze. His hands relaxed. And laugh lines creased his face.

I plucked the fabric of my blouse away from my suddenly overheated skin as I fought to remember what we were talking about.

"Uh." My tongue didn't want to work. I tried again. "She's out there. Piper. With the people."

His lips twitched.

I brushed a thumb along my lower lip, just in case I was drooling, and reminded myself the man was totally not my type. "I waved to her on the way in."

"I'll have one of my guys bring her over. How will they recognize her?"

Did that mean he was going to send Detective Locke, or did Detective Watson count as one of the guys? "She has presence."

He waited a beat. "Maybe you should tell me what she looks like."

Sure, because with all the people gathering out there, finding Piper by her hair color wouldn't be harder than finding her energy. I bit my lip to stop the giggles that suddenly wanted to escape. When I was sure I was under control, I tried to give him just the basics. "Brown hair. Huge brown eyes. She likes to be involved in everything, so if they call her name, she'll find them."

Detective Just-The-Basics nodded without looking at me as he relayed the information to someone on the other end of a walkie-talkie.

Why did he need a walkie-talkie? He was practically glued to his phone.

As if to prove my point, he started looking at something on his phone and typing notes or texts or something, completely ignoring me.

Did that mean I was free to go? I shifted, and his eyes snapped to my face.

Before either of us could say anything, there were voices outside, and the sound of feet hurrying up the wooden steps and across the deck.

I could almost believe the door opened itself to

get out of Piper's way as she burst in. Then my best friend stood just inside the door, taking in the scene.

Whatever she saw made her pause. "Where's Kerri?"

The detective gave me a what's-she-talking-about look.

"My lawyer," I explained before turning back to Piper. "I haven't been arrested."

"What do you mean, you haven't been arrested? You always get arrested."

Detective Let's-Get-Down-To-Business cleared his throat. "Ms. Fields, if you could wait outside, this shouldn't take long."

"You want to speak with me?" Piper's eyelashes fluttered briefly as she glanced between us.

He nodded. "Have a seat."

I pushed to my feet and offered her my chair. "I'll just be outside, then."

I moved toward the door slowly, trying hard not to throw my hands in the air.

What can I say? Old habits die hard.

I stepped outside and pulled the door almost closed. The man who'd escorted Piper to the security office was just disappearing around the bend.

After another quick glance around to make sure no one was paying attention, I pressed my back against the wall beside the door.

If anyone caught me, I could just pretend I was weak after the ordeal of finding a body and needed the wall's support. Since Hector and his team hadn't bothered to get out the chairs that spent the summer on the deck, what else was I supposed to do?

As far as excuses went, it was a weak one, but it was all I had.

"What can I do for you?" Piper's voice squeezed through the crack in the door. She sounded light and airy, as if she didn't have a care in the world. "I'm sorry, what was your name?"

I grinned. Maybe I should find a window to spy through. I didn't want to miss Piper taking a bite out of the detective. Except then, even though I'd be able to see, I wouldn't hear anything.

"Detective Price." He cleared his throat again.

Piper had that effect on most men. "I'm Piper Holland."

"Ms. Holland, I just need to confirm that Ludwig Baylor was in the violin shop when you arrived, and that you remained there until Ms. Fields came down to the amphitheater."

"Did something happen to Ludwig? Or was it his violin? Did something happen to his Gagliano?" Piper paused, then went on in a rush. "You can't think Octavia had anything to do with whatever's happened. She would never damage an instrument, no matter who it belonged to. Octavia wouldn't hurt a fly."

Well, maybe a fly. Certainly a mosquito. But I'd feel bad about cutting its life short.

"Ms. Holland." The detective's voice was enough to cut off Piper's diatribe. "Just answer the question."

"I was with Octavia from the time Ludwig left until she went to meet Tatiana. She was running late, of course, but everyone expects that with Octavia."

I couldn't even take offense at that. It was absolutely true. My *creative application of time* was one of the big reasons I wasn't asked to show up for events anymore.

"Thank you, Ms. Holland. If I need anything else, someone from my team will reach out to you."

"You aren't going to arrest her, are you?"

The pause that followed her question was long enough to make me wonder if Detective Price was going to change his mind.

When he spoke, his voice had a gruff edge to it. "I have no desire to arrest Octavia."

A tingle ran through me at the way he said my name. I frowned and pressed my hand into my stomach. I had no business getting excited at the way he said my name. If ever there was a person who wasn't my type, it was this man. He was a—a—a law enforcer!

Nope, I wasn't interested. And obviously, he wasn't, either. Law enforcers don't like people who get arrested as often as I do. That was fine. Fine. I was adjusting to being single again, that's all. Morton and I had only called it quits a few weeks ago. I hadn't even told Piper about the breakup yet.

Of course, I'd only seen her for a few minutes, and we hadn't been alone. Breakup stories were more of a one-on-one activity than a share-it-with-your-employees kind of thing.

And Piper! She was supposed to be working her charm on the detective. He wasn't even clearing his throat anymore.

"Maybe you don't want to arrest her, but are you going to anyway?" Piper sounded curious. Maybe she was just drawing him in slowly.

"I'll follow every lead. Including confirming your alibi."

"Mine?"

"Octavia—Ms. Fields—made it clear she believes you're innocent." Detective Skeptical didn't sound like he believed me. "For now, the alibi she gave you checks out."

"I'm a suspect?" She didn't have to sound so thrilled. "I've never been a suspect before. My husband will think I'm making it up. What did I maybe do?"

He hesitated.

Come on, Detective Tight-Lipped, if you don't tell her, I will.

Maybe he heard my thought, or maybe he decided he could trust her. "Octavia and the head of security found the body of Ludwig Baylor. While it's possible his death was an accident—"

"He was murdered."

"That's what I'm trying to ascertain."

A chair creaked, and I imagined Piper tossing

her Marilyn Monroe hair as she leaned back and crossed her legs. "Good luck with narrowing down your suspects. Everyone hated that man."

"Can you be more specific?"

"I'm telling you, there isn't a person in that symphony who liked Ludwig. Octavia was nicer to him than anyone else, and that's only because she believes in peace and love and letting everyone live their own best life." The chair creaked again. "Ludwig was in rare form at rehearsal this morning. We were practicing for the season's opening concert tomorrow, and Ludwig didn't think people were taking it seriously enough."

I almost stuck my head in the door to point out that people expect that from him, but then I remembered I wasn't actually part of the conversation.

Piper continued, completely unaware I'd almost interrupted. "You want suspects, get a copy of the symphony roster. He was yelling so much that Tatiana went nose-to-nose with him and told him he was a terrible leader, and that the only reason he got the concertmaster position was because he schmoozed the board members."

"Is it true?"

"Probably." Piper's dainty sniff was loud enough she could have been standing next to me. "Tatiana was right. Ludwig's never been a good leader. Mostly we ignore him, but lately he's been going out of his way to force us into respecting him."

That was the first I'd heard of him wanting

respect that badly. Then again, I didn't usually pay attention to that kind of thing.

"This is the same woman Octavia was supposed to be meeting?" Detective Price asked.

I looked at the bow case I'd forgotten I was holding, my mind spinning.

Tatiana was supposed to be at the amphitheater, but I hadn't see any sign of her. Yes, I was late, but as Piper said, people were used to my flexible relationship with time. If Tatiana wanted that bow right away, she either would have waited for me or come to the shop. If she'd come to the shop, she would have passed me on the way, because there was only one path cut into the mountainside.

Something told me Tatiana was about to be dealing with her own questioning.

The sound of a chair scraping back had me tiptoeing away from the door. By the time they stepped outside I was at the end of the deck, gripping the wood with my toes as I stretched tall, trying to see the activity over at the amphitheater.

Piper swooped over to pull me into a hug. "You poor thing. It's been an exciting afternoon for you."

I didn't know how to reply, which was fine, because Piper didn't give me the chance to say anything before propelling me over to where the detective stood, his intent eyes taking in everything.

I wiped my suddenly sweaty palms on the seat of my shorts.

Was he thinking that it was convenient for two friends to alibi each other like this? Did we mention there were other people who could confirm where we were? Xavier, and Mairi, and Eli had all been in the room with us, and Jamie—another one of the instrument repair guys—would have heard us when Eli opened the door.

Or were they not good references, since they technically worked for me?

No. The detective had told me I wasn't a suspect, and that if Piper's story confirmed mine, she wouldn't be one, either.

Choosing to trust a cop wasn't exactly a natural thing for me, but I could do it if I tried.

Detective Confusing nodded at us. "Thank you for your time, ladies. That's all for now. If I have any other questions, I know where to find you."

Piper thanked him and started to lead me away.

The scene from the greenroom popped into my head and I slowed, turning back to find the detective still watching us. "What's going to happen to Ludwig's violin?"

He shrugged. "I suppose it will go into the evidence locker."

"What?" Piper gasped as her hand reached up to her throat as if she was trying to grasp a pearl necklace, which showed exactly how horrified she was.

That woman hasn't worn pearls a day in her life. They're totally not her vibe.

"You can't put a Gagliano in lockup," I argued. Piper seemed to have lost the ability to say anything, and someone had to.

"It's not exactly prison." Detective Price gave me one of *those* looks. The kind that said he wasn't sure if he should be taking me seriously. "I'm sure it will be safe."

"Tell him." Piper pushed me toward him. "Tell him he can't do that."

Five

I STUMBLED FORWARD A STEP as Piper pushed on the back of my shoulder again.

Detective Price's hand twitched, almost as if he were going to reach out to steady me, but then it fell back to his side.

I was going to have to convince him, a man who clearly wasn't a musician and didn't understand the needs of such an old, exquisite instrument, that placing the violin in some room to be ignored and forgotten about was a crime.

Like he'd listen to me. Still, for the Gagliano's sake, I had to try. "Is it climate controlled? Humidity, temperature, all that?"

He shrugged.

"How long will it be there? Do you know to make sure the bow is loosened? Or—"

"Ms. Fields."

"—that it can't be right next to an air vent, or—"

"Octavia," Detective Price tried again.

This time my words died.

He gave me a reassuring look. "They handle all kinds of things. I'm sure they'll figure it out."

"You don't understand. This is a Gagliano. It can't be locked away like that."

Detective Stubborn didn't seem to understand what I was trying so desperately to explain.

"The violin is worth a lot of money," Piper said. She crossed her arms and cocked a hip. "You wouldn't want to be held responsible for any damage, would you?"

I waited as he typed something into his phone. With any luck, he wasn't asking for backup to help with the crazy ladies who cared so much about something he clearly didn't understand.

After a minute, he looked up from the screen. "I assume you have some other place in mind to store the instrument?"

"Octavia has an instrument safe in her shop," Piper volunteered. "You should keep it there."

While I wanted to distance myself from this investigation—I'd already participated more than I'd ever have expected—I couldn't let that violin go sit in some warehouse or whatever. "I do. It's empty right now."

"Fine. But you don't let anyone so much as open that safe until I come back for it."

"I suppose I could change the combination so my staff can't open it." I couldn't help feeling like agreeing to this was a bad idea. I mean, of course I wanted the violin somewhere safe, and a safe in a violin shop was better than anything else the detective had come up with, but—

"It's settled." Piper spun around, her natural stage presence turning the move into something dramatic and impressive, and started down the path. "Let's go get the violin and make sure it's secured."

Detective Price shook his head a tiny bit.

Clearly he wasn't used to being handled by a woman like Piper. Hardly anyone was.

I shrugged. "Okay, then."

As we followed after her, the detective glanced at the ground. "Did you lose your shoes at the crime scene? I'm sorry I didn't notice sooner. I'll make sure you get them back."

I followed his gaze to my bare toes. "Oh. No. I mean, they aren't at—" I tried not to stumble over the words "—the crime scene."

He waited.

I clamped my lips together. I hated it when cops played that trick. Someone eventually had to say something, and if it was me, they got to win.

Thirty-one steps later, he caved. "Do you need shoes?"

A part of me wanted to be offended, but the quiet concern in his voice made me smile instead. "I have shoes. I just don't wear them unless I have to."

"Okay." Detective Surprisingly-Sincere was actually trying to understand. He clearly didn't know the joy of digging toes into soil, but he wasn't judging me, either, which was more than I could say for most of the people I knew.

What would he say if I told him the earth played her own music, and if you were still enough you could feel it through your feet?

He'd think I was crazy.

Still, a part of me hoped that maybe someday I'd be able to teach him to feel Mother Earth's heartbeat.

I looked away before I could do something stupid and try to teach him about it when he had other things to be doing.

The cluster of people watching the proceedings at the amphitheater had grown. Every office and practice room must have emptied, and the musicians who were moving into their summer apartments had decided to finish settling in later.

"How long will you keep the amphitheater closed?" I wondered out loud as we caught up with Piper, who was busy waving at everyone she knew just so they'd know she was privy to information they didn't have.

Detective Price walked a little faster. "We should have everything we need shortly, but I might keep it taped off until morning."

"Rehearsal is scheduled for nine in the morning," Piper offered. "Two hours, plus the dress rehearsal in the afternoon before the concert tomorrow evening."

It shouldn't have surprised me that the concert would still be happening, but it did.

Piper read that in my expression. "Oh, Octavia, you know they can't cancel it. They've sold tickets for the dress rehearsal, and the concert's been sold out for ages. Besides, once word gets out about Ludwig, there will be an even bigger rush for tickets for concerts and rehearsals for the rest of the season."

There was nothing to say to that. If Detective Price said the amphitheater could be used, the symphony couldn't risk postponing the concert or refunding the tickets, even though any loss of sales would be made up for by people who only came because of the death.

No one wanted to hear that the aura of the place was tainted, or that Ludwig's spirit should be laid to rest before life went on.

The whole situation was a downer, and the worst part was that there was nothing I could do about it.

Death was an inevitable part of life.

Maybe I could convince Hector to let me smudge the greenroom to cleanse the air before everyone was allowed back in.

"You've got that look in your eye," Piper said.

Detective Curious turned to study me. "What look?"

"She's going to go hippie-dippie on us." From most people, that would sound condescending, but Piper spoke with the affection of someone who at least accepted the *hippie-dippie* stuff, even if they didn't believe in it.

Nope. Not a chance. I shook my head. I'd wait and let my freak flag fly with Hector. Time to change the subject. "I was just wondering if you're going to have someone bring the violin out, or if we're going in to get it."

Detective Price tipped his head toward the benches. "Go sit where I found you. I'll bring it out myself."

He disappeared, and Piper and I made our way over to sit down.

Piper fanned herself. "That is one fine detective."

I wasn't going to take the bait, even if the man was something to behold. Piper could wait and swoon over him with Xavier.

"I've always loved a man with broad shoulders."

Nope, she still wasn't going to get me. Besides, the man's shoulders and muscles weren't the most attractive part of him. There was kindness in his eyes, and his aura was something most people could spend their whole lives working toward and not get close to.

"Do you think all those people are going to hang around until the investigators leave?" I asked, glancing back at the onlookers.

"Once they see Detective Price, they will."

I shook my head. "You have a one-track mind, Piper. You didn't really even flirt with him."

She tapped the back of my hand with a single, long finger. "That's because he didn't want to flirt with me."

When had that ever stopped her?

The detective in question came out carrying Ludwig's violin case with the same care he'd give a bomb. He held it out in front of me.

I took the case and draped the strap over my shoulder.

He looked relieved to be rid of the responsibility. "I'll escort you both to the shop."

Piper made a sound halfway between a choke and a purr.

The detective ignored her, so I did, too.

"We'll change the safe's combination to something only the two of us know." His eyes narrowed a fraction. "That way, if this evidence is tampered with, I know exactly where to look."

Rude.

So much for thinking Detective Smart-Alec was starting to trust me.

Six

"EVERYONE WAS TALKING ABOUT IT, of course." Piper draped herself over the display case. "No one seems to know anything beyond what Detective Price told me."

The only reason anyone knew that much was because Piper was terrible at keeping anything to herself.

Okay, there were times she managed it, but only because she cared enough about her friends not to broadcast every tiny irrelevant thing.

But the fact that all the musicians spent the time sandwiching their morning rehearsal talking about the death of one of their own was to be expected, especially when no one knew how or why he died.

True to his word, Detective Price had released his hold on the amphitheater first thing in the morning, which meant the symphony was free to hold their rehearsals as scheduled.

Piper tapped my hand, as if her being directly across from me wasn't enough to make sure she had my attention. "When are you going to share the details?"

"What details? I don't know anything."

Her laugh filled the room.

From the corner of my eye, I noticed Mairi turn with a frown from where she was fussing with a metronome display on the other side of the room.

Oops. I'd forgotten I was supposed to try to keep Piper from leaving fingerprints all over the glass.

Not that her fingers were touching the glass, but her elbows and forearms were, and for some reason, Mairi counted any smears or marks on the glass as fingerprints.

Not that anyone else seemed bothered by a few fingerprints, elbow prints, or any other kind of prints.

"You must know something juicy." Piper prompted. "You were there."

And I'd spent a sleepless night in my tiny house loft bed trying not to think about it. "What were people saying?"

She blew her bangs out of her eyes. "Everyone knows you found Ludwig. And that the detectives were interested in getting your help in learning who might have a grudge against him."

That would explain all the smiles and waves I'd received as I'd pedaled my bicycle up the path toward the shop this morning. A lot of musicians I barely knew had greeted me as we passed each other.

I was used to staring, but it was usually because

people thought I was strange, not because they were trying to show me they had nothing to hide.

"What else?" I asked.

Piper's eyes sparkled. "The idea that I'm a suspect is circulating."

"You're not a suspect anymore."

"Po-tay-to, po-tah-to. That detective might have said my alibi checked out, but I bet my picture is hanging on a murder board back at his office." She bounced with excitement. "You're never fully ruled out until the real killer is caught."

I took her by the shoulders and pushed her off the display case. The thing was anchored to the floor, but that didn't mean it couldn't break if she bounced too energetically. I might take that in stride, but Mairi and Xavier would have a fit.

"Aren't you excited to be a suspect?" Piper asked.

"Why, so they could lock me up again?" I tried not to imagine Detective Dreamy locking me in a cell where he'd have to see me again.

"To be fair, you've never been locked up for murder. Maybe it's different."

I laughed. I couldn't help it.

You heard me talking with the detective, so you won't be surprised that I have a record. But it's not like I had an arrest wall with an empty spot waiting for a murder charge.

"I'm not really interested in a murder charge, but thanks for thinking of me." I fiddled with the display of strings beside me so it would make more sense. My employees had grouped them all by brand, but if they were divided by instrument, people who used a mix would find things easier.

I couldn't be the only person who mixed and matched. In my experience, very few serious musicians didn't have some variety to the strings on their instrument.

Piper pulled out her phone to check the time.

"I don't know why you insist on carrying that thing around." We'd had the argument before, but I knew Piper would see it as a cue that I didn't want to talk about the murder anymore.

"They're convenient." Piper pushed it back into her purse. "Are you sure you don't want to talk about Ludwig? I know you didn't sleep last night, your eyes have shadows a mile long. Talking about it might help you work through it."

Work through what? I found the body of a person who I'd once considered a friend, back before his head had grown so large. There was nothing to work through. Nothing at all.

"I've got five minutes before I have to leave for dress rehearsal. What should we talk about instead?" Piper pretended to think.

The look in her eyes made me squirm, and I didn't know why. "You could tell me something about your trip."

"There isn't time to do it justice. But I did hear something interesting. There's a rumor going around that one of the concerts next week has a last-minute change in conductor because someone bowed out."

Oh. That.

I grabbed a fist full of hair and tossed it behind my shoulder, pretending like I didn't know exactly what she was getting at. "Really? That's strange."

"Out with it, Octavia. Why did Morton cancel? He pulled strings to get this concert."

"We haven't talked about it." With any luck, that would hold her off for a while. I knew I needed to explain what had happened, why Morton and I had split, but I needed more than a hurried five minutes before rehearsal.

And we should probably wait until we could talk about it at my place so Mairi wasn't listening in— she was sure to tell Xavier, if Piper didn't beat her to it, and I was trying to keep a sliver of professional distance with my employees.

Not that Xavier and Mairi were good at keeping any of that distance themselves. At least there was professional distance with the repair guys, if only because Jamie and Eli didn't care what was going on in the rest of the shop, as long as they were left in peace.

"Octavia."

I sighed. "Not right now, Piper. You don't want to be late to rehearsal."

Her eyes widened in alarm. "You never worry about time."

"Go."

She hesitated. "What are you doing after the concert tonight?"

A chill crept down my spine as I considered the

way I'd spent the previous night. "Sleeping, I hope."

"Okay, that's a good idea. Get rid of those tired eyes before the detective comes back." Piper leaned across the display case to give me a quick hug. "Before you sleep, you're coming to the bonfire with me."

I loved the opening night bonfire. The musicians who were staying in the on-site apartments hosted the party for the rest of the symphony, and it was always spectacular.

"You'll have fun, I promise. You need to get your mind off Ludwig's murder for a while. Maybe it will help you sleep better tonight." Piper picked up her violin case and pulled the strap over her shoulder. "I'm not taking no for an answer. You're coming."

"How much blood was there?"

"Is it true you're helping figure out what happened?"

One of the violinists I hadn't met before pushed closer. "Did he suffer? He deserved to suffer a little bit."

"We're the ones who suffered, putting up with him for so long."

I pushed the glasses up my nose. I pretended I could see the happy fires and tables of food past the group of curious musicians around me as I tried to decide if I should answer any questions.

Detective I'm-In-Charge had told me it would be best if I didn't talk about it—except maybe to a professional—but I didn't want people thinking I really was helping with the investigation.

I wasn't investigating. That kind of thing would weigh a person down, and I didn't need that responsibility.

Not that the symphony members crowding my personal space understood that.

"Can you see me as an investigator?" I laughed as I gestured at my embroidered overall shorts and bare feet.

"What did he look like?"

I bit the inside of my cheek and tried not to laugh at the guy's eagerness. You'd think the area was full of kindergarteners, not full-grown, serious musicians.

Well, maybe not *serious* musicians the way you're probably imagining.

The music pouring from wireless speakers showed a different side of the group. The straitlaced audience members who'd gone into raptures listening to these musicians perform Mozart and Brahms would have been all disapproving frowns if they heard the heavy bass and crooning artists that graced the playlist.

I'm not saying it was Woodstock, but even the stodgiest musician had kicked back. Literally. He was on the edge of the clearing, sitting in the dirt with his ankles crossed in front of him, leaning against the trunk of a tree.

He'd probably regret that when he noticed the sap stains his white button-down was accumulating.

"Octavia?"

I startled. What had they been saying? "I'm sorry, I really can't talk about it."

Hopefully that would keep people from asking too many more questions. It wasn't that I was bowing to the detective's wishes—Ha! Can you imagine?—but the sooner we all stopped talking about it, the sooner things could get back to normal.

I liked normal.

Fine, normal was overrated, but when you're going to break from normal it shouldn't have to be for a murder.

"Was it really murder?" a quiet voice asked.

Had I been thinking out loud again? No, someone would have snorted at the idea of me and normal being in the same sentence instead of jumping on the murder thing. "You'd have to ask Detective Price about that. Excuse me, I need a drink."

I swerved around clusters of people as I made a beeline for the picnic table covered in drinks and coolers. When I got there, Austin—the timpanist who liked to play bartender—was already holding out a lemonade.

Yes, lemonade.

Tipping it toward him in a silent toast, I dropped onto the bench beside him.

"You had some excitement," he offered as he

handed a drink to someone else. No, not lemonade—that was only for me. The rest of the people here didn't seem to care they were poisoning their bodies. "Are you okay?"

"Yeah." Or I would be, anyway, once I stopped seeing Ludwig sprawled on the floor every time I closed my eyes. "It's just . . . trippy."

Austin nodded as if he truly understood, then took a deep breath. "Listen, Octavia, there's something you should know."

Ugh. I hated it when people said there was something I should know. It almost always meant I wouldn't like what I heard. You know, like when someone says we need to talk.

I tried to steel myself, but the music was wrapping me in warmth, and the dancing light from four—yes, four—large fires made me want to dance, too. "What?"

"Ludwig was causing problems."

As if that was news. Ludwig adored causing problems. I snorted into my lemonade. "More than normal?"

Austin handed out another drink, then turned back to me. He leaned in close and spoke quietly into my ear. "Ludwig was a character, but lately his ego was taking over more than normal."

I nodded. Anyone could see that.

"When I stopped at the housing office yesterday to get my housing assignment and key, Ludwig was there. He stormed out just as I went in." Austin pulled away to pour a drink and laugh with the principal flautist, then his lips were back at my ear. "It was clear something had gone down. The housing staff was tense, and no one would even look at me."

As sorry as I felt for the housing staff, explosions were something you dealt with where Ludwig was concerned. "Why are you telling me this?"

He shrugged. "I thought you'd want to know. You know, since you're helping the police with their investigation."

I rolled my eyes. Since when does finding the body of someone you knew, then being questioned by Detective I-Know-What-I'm-Doing mean a person is helping with an investigation? "Detective Price is perfectly capable, I'm sure. His team doesn't need my help, even if I wanted to give it to them."

"If Ludwig had a friend, it was you."

Not exactly true.

Sure, once upon a time we'd gotten along, but that was *before*.

Before I was friendly with his now-ex-wife.

Before I saw through that professional front to the insecurity beneath the perfectly cultivated inflated ego.

Before I was asked to leave the symphony.

Honestly, I think it was that last one that did in our tentative friendship. Ludwig was horrified I couldn't seem to manage to live my life around the symphony's schedule, and—well, there's no need to go into what he did from there. I don't need that kind of karma.

Austin pulled back, straightening my glasses as he did. "Whether you're helping them or not, I'm sure you'll have a better idea what to do with the information than I do."

A group approached the picnic table and Austin turned to help them.

Taking what was left of my lemonade, I wandered over to the semi-darkness of the surrounding trees. The music washed over me. I closed my eyes and started to sway.

"Octavia, there you are."

I sighed. I'd know that voice anywhere, even without the hint of an Eastern European accent that had almost disappeared in the decade the woman had been in the country. I opened my eyes. "Tatiana."

"You didn't bring my bow." She tossed her head. Her spiked pixie cut, dyed bright red, didn't move.

What did she put in her hair to keep it so stiff? Or was that a natural thing? My hair hung past my waist and hadn't been shorter than mid-back since I was seven, so it was a mystery to me.

"Where is it?"

I stopped looking at her hair. "I took your bow to the amphitheater yesterday, just like we talked about."

"You were supposed to bring it to the apartment." Her eyes flicked in the direction of the buildings as if she could see them through the trees.

I should have known she'd twist things so I was the bad guy. I smiled my best bubblehead smile. "The delivery instructions were written on the repair tag, Tatiana. I can show you, if you'd like."

"Bring it tomorrow."

"You can pick it up any time after we open." I avoided her glare by looking up at the stars, so bright without the lights of the city.

"You said you'd bring it to me." Tatiana's voice twisted with the start of a whine. "You must keep your word."

"I kept my word. I took your bow to the amphitheater, where you were supposed to meet me." I let my gaze lower until I was staring at her. "Funny thing. Instead of finding you waiting in the greenroom to meet me, I found Ludwig."

She blinked, but her fist opened and closed at her side. "I had nothing to do with that."

Now, normally I don't let people bait me. I try not to get involved in things that could damage my zen. So the words that came out of my mouth next weren't just a surprise to Tatiana, they surprised me as well. "But you did tell him he was a terrible leader and didn't deserve to be concertmaster, didn't you? And so close to when he died. Hmm. I wonder what those detectives would make of that."

"I told you, I had nothing to do with it." Tatiana sounded a little rattled. She took a deep breath. "What I said, it was true. He was a miserable little man who was nothing without his job. I was to meet with the board about him. I was going to tell them how Ludwig abused his role, and that we all want a new concertmaster who will do the job properly. I didn't have to kill him—I was going to get him fired."

Seven

TATIANA'S WORDS RANG IN MY ears as I pedaled my bicycle away from Aerie Pines. The winding road was empty, and peaceful after the noise of the party.

I was trying to let my mind wander through all the things I'd heard at the party—and let me tell you, there was a lot—but somehow I kept coming back to Tatiana.

Why would a person try to get a co-worker fired? Didn't that say more about the person filing the complaint than it did about the person who might lose their job?

Knowing Tatiana had been planning to throw Ludwig under the bus like that should have convinced me she couldn't have killed him. Instead, it made me more suspicious of her than I'd been to begin with.

Because really, Tatiana could be nice to people who weren't me, so I hadn't imagined she was actually a suspect. And despite what she said at the bonfire, she knew exactly where we were supposed to meet.

Could Detective Doesn't-Actually-Know-The-Players be looking at Tatiana seriously? Piper had told him about Tatiana's argument with Ludwig.

But then there was the tension Austin had felt in the housing office. Tatiana couldn't have caused that. She wasn't even there.

I turned my handlebars and cut across the road to start up the gravel driveway winding through the underbrush. After about a quarter of a mile or so, the gravel gave way to packed dirt and the road opened to a large clearing.

Hopping off Clover—yes, of course I named my bike—I leaned her against my scrappy little camper van—yes, I named that, too, her name is Betty—and scooped my shoes out of Clover's basket.

Look, just because I don't wear them doesn't mean I don't take them to Aerie Pines with me just in case.

Although maybe it would be easier if I just left them in the office at the violin shop.

I pulled a flannel shirt off the back of a camp chair on my way across the clearing and climbed the two steps to the itty-bitty deck of my tiny house, opened the door, and dumped the shirt on the chair just inside so I had a free hand to turn on the light.

I'm not gonna lie. My tiny house on wheels looked like the kind of gypsy caravan you'd see in an old movie. The arched inside was purple and blue and magenta, with bright pops of yellow. Protection symbols were painted on the lintels and a sparkly bead curtain was draped back from the door, but the round windows were bare and usually left open wide. The fabrics on the chairs, table linens, and the bedding up in the little sleeping loft were all rich jewel-toned velvet and silk with gold and silver trim.

I tossed my shoes into the shoe basket on the tiny deck, then closed the door.

Normally I'd build a fire in the pit outside, or sit and relax with a drink or snack before catching some z's, but I was exhausted. I swallowed a quick glass of water, then climbed the ladder and collapsed on the bed. Right over my head was a roof window—yes, I know most people call them skylights, but roof window sounds better—and I watched the treetops swaying against the backdrop of stars until I drifted off.

When a quiet chittering woke me, the sky had turned the red and orange of early morning.

The chittering got louder as I rustled the bedding.

I rolled onto my side. "Morning, Frenzy."

My visitor was on the edge of the bed, his back legs stretched out behind him while his front legs were bent. His little squirrel hands clutched a nut. He blinked at me and chittered again.

"Did I oversleep?" I asked.

Frenzy offered a little whistle in reply, then went back to gnawing on the nut.

He had the right idea. I reached for my glasses and climbed down to find something to fill my own belly.

As I got ready for the day—I chose a patchwork skirt that hit just above the knees and an eyelet peasant top—I realized that sometime in the night, I'd made a decision.

I was going to have to tell Detective Price about my conversations with Tatiana and Austin.

Stepping outside, I closed my eyes and took a deep breath of the clean mountain air. I missed it during the winter, but that was my time for wandering adventures.

I made my way toward Clover, my mind replaying that final conversation I'd had with Ludwig. When I got to the part about his ex-wife, I stopped in my tracks.

Would anyone have contacted Cora? She and Ludwig were divorced. I had no idea what that meant in a situation like this, but she probably didn't count as next-of-kin anymore.

Someone had to make sure she knew, if only because of the kids.

I moved Clover aside and climbed into Betty. The key fell from its place in the visor—right next to where my driver's license lived—and I stuck it in the ignition. "Time to wake up, girl."

It took two tries, but the engine turned over with a roar. I trundled down the driveway and turned toward Aerie Pines. Not that my employees would mind if I didn't show up, but it seemed like a good idea to let them know where I was going.

When I let myself into the shop, everything was quiet. A glance at the clock in the office told me I was early for once. Mairi and Xavier wouldn't be in for a couple of hours. I grabbed a pen and paper off the desk.

> Have to go down the mountain for a bit. Be back this afternoon. Oh, and can one of you call Detective Price and let him know I need to talk to him?
>
> 8[via]

Taping the note to the door where they couldn't miss it, I turned and made my way back to the parking lot.

After an uneventful trip down the canyon and across the valley, I wound my way through the city to the narrow street where Cora lived. I left Betty on the side of the road and climbed the stairs to the fifth floor apartment.

Cora opened the door after the first knock. "Octavia. What—what are you doing here?"

Now, I'm not one who cares how people look, but poor Cora looked so frazzled and strung out that she desperately needed an aura cleanse.

"Aren't you supposed to be up at that music complex place?"

Commune. Complex. What was it with people feeling like they needed to put a label on the place? And if it needed a label, why couldn't they go with community, or campus? They're all C words. Practically interchangeable.

I pulled myself back from where my thoughts were leading. "I've been there for a few days, but I came to see you."

This was harder than I'd expected. How did you tell someone their ex-husband was dead?

I grabbed a fistful of hair and tossed it over my shoulder. Maybe I should have suggested Detective Price handle this.

No, Cora needed a friendly face.

"You heard about Ludwig." Cora's shoulders dropped. "What am I saying? Of course you did. You're up there where it happened."

Relief flooded me. I would have done it, really, but a tiny part of me was glad someone had gotten there before me. I didn't want to be responsible for breaking her. "I did. Are you okay?"

That was a terrible question. Of course she wasn't okay. She'd loved Ludwig, once.

Cora opened the door wider and motioned for me to come in.

I stepped into the small living room and immediately turned down the drink Cora offered. I hadn't come to do anything but offer support.

Pushing Lego bricks aside with her foot, Cora led me over to the couch. "Sorry about the mess. I'm hardly ever home long enough to clean up."

"What's the point in cleaning up when they're just going to get the toys out again?" I'd never understood the need to put things away when they were going to be used every day. Although I suppose it was easier to find things if they'd been put away.

Cora's smile was weary. "Have you heard if it's been ruled an accident?"

"I haven't heard anything official since it first happened. But there are homicide detectives involved, so I'm guessing that means they don't think it was an accident."

Cora was quiet for a bit. "I got a call from someone on the symphony board this morning. They want to do a memorial concert."

"That's really nice of them." I wondered what politics had gone into working that out. The concert schedule had been planned for a long time.

She nodded. "Apparently one of the conductors had to back out at the last minute. The board decided to bring in someone Ludwig had been pushing them to hire as an associate conductor. They'll use the concert as an audition to see if they want to work him into the rotation of up-and-comers trying to get the job. And they're changing the music to some of Ludwig's favorites."

I guess Morton canceling worked out for everyone, then. "Will you be at the concert?" With any luck the board wouldn't drag her up on the stage to accept some kind of tribute. I didn't want anyone to give Cora a hard time.

"I haven't decided yet. It's all so strange." She sank into the couch, looking lost. "Ludwig is—there was so much life in him, especially after the divorce. I can hardly believe he's gone. The kids are devastated. He promised to let them go stay at Aerie Pines with him for a couple of weeks."

He was going to take the kids up there? Don't get me wrong, I think the mountains are a wonderful place for kids. But Aerie Pines didn't have anything set up for them. No playgrounds, or adventures, or even a daycare. Some of the musicians brought entire families, but they had a spouse—or in a couple of cases I knew of, a nanny—to take the kids on adventures while the musicians were busy.

What was he expecting his kids to do while he was in rehearsals and concerts? Because not even Ludwig would expect kids to sit quietly for two weeks.

"Everyone must be devastated," Cora continued. "It's such a loss for the symphony."

I made a non-comital sound. It was probably best if she remembered him in a good light.

"It must have been so hard for the musicians to walk in for rehearsal and find him there." She bit her lip and her eyes welled up with tears.

I shifted uneasily. Surely, if someone had told her Ludwig was gone, they'd also explained how he'd been found. "His body was discovered before anyone could go for practice."

"Really?" Confusion clouded her face. "The officer who visited didn't mention that. Who found him?"

"I did."

Eight

IT WAS A RELIEF WHEN my shop came into view. I leaned Clover against the back of the building, then followed the stream along the side of the shop and across the path to the pond. Well, I called it a pond. Everyone else said it was a small lake. Either way, my shop was the only one with a clear view of the peaceful water.

Walking around the pond wouldn't take long, and it would help settle me before going into the shop.

It turns out that learning someone you know—and are, well, friendly with—found the body of your ex-husband and is now sitting next to you leads to all sorts of stressful questions. Who knew, right?

When I saw Tatiana come out of the shop, I decided it was time for me to go help out. Xavier and Mairi shouldn't have to deal with all the problems.

I made my way inside. "I'm back. Sorry you had to take care of Tatiana alone."

Xavier pursed his lips. "She's perfectly lovely when you aren't here to needle her."

Mairi finished her fanatical polishing of the glass case. "Don't touch the displays. We finally finished organizing them."

I looked around. They had indeed finished unpacking the boxes and setting up the shop. "But I had the strings organized by instrument."

Xavier clucked his tongue. "This works better. If you change it, no one will be able to find anything."

He was wrong, of course. Doing it my way would make things easier to find. But I knew better than to mess with the two of them when they ganged up on me like this.

I changed the topic. "Did you call the detective?"

"Not directly, no. But Mairi left a message for him at the station." Xavier removed a bit of non-existent fluff from his shirt and dropped the imaginary thing into the trash can. "You could have done as much."

"I don't have a phone." I pretended the shop phone in the office didn't count. And even if I had my own phone, I wouldn't have made the call. People were meant to talk to each other in person, not through whatever made phones work. But if other people were okay with that, I saw nothing wrong with letting them do it on my behalf. "What's been happening today?"

Mairi rattled off a list of people who came in, and what they'd bought, punctuated with Xavier's stories about the real reason they were here—wanting to know what was happening with the Ludwig Case, as he called it—and what tidbits of their own they'd let slip.

"Did you know everyone in the symphony has to reaudition at the end of the summer? Something about contracts." Xavier planted a hand on his hip. "Piper mentioned it when she came in to check on you, assuming you'd be here."

I tried not to look at the strings that were calling to be reorganized as I nodded. "The symphony used to be a community thing that anyone could participate in. Eventually they went to auditions, and once it became a paying job they needed contracts. Someone decided redoing all the contracts at once would be easier than staggering them."

"That makes no sense. Ooooo." Xavier's voice did that thing that gave away his intense interest at possible new gossip. "And who is this?"

Mairi frowned. "I don't know."

Glad for any excuse to move my attention away from all the things I wanted to rearrange, I angled toward the window. The blond hair and suit gave away the man's identity before I saw his face. "That would be Detective Price."

"That's the detective?" Mairi's voice sounded strange. Breathy.

"You didn't say he looked like that," Xavier whispered as the detective reached for the glass door. "No wonder you wanted to talk to him again."

I bit the inside of my cheek and tried to keep my face blank. For good measure, I moved behind the counter and started looking through the receipts. "It's not like that."

Xavier didn't reply, but only because the detective was halfway inside.

I swear the air changed when Detective Price sauntered in. It was harder to breathe somehow.

Detective Full-Of-Himself stopped directly across from me and leaned on the display case, his palm pressed against the glass.

I glanced at Mairi. Her lips were parted, but she didn't seem at all concerned about the smudges being deposited on her clean glass.

Detective Price's unwavering gaze pulled my eyes back to him. "Fifty-seven."

I swallowed. "Is that supposed to mean something?"

"It's the number of times you've been arrested." His face remained impassive.

Xavier, on the other hand, pressed his hand against his chest as he gasped.

"Oh." I bit my lip. Maybe it would be better to have this conversation somewhere else. Anywhere my employees weren't able to eavesdrop.

Not that they had any delusions about who I was.

Detective Pay-Attention cleared his throat. "Do you protest everything?"

I thought for a few seconds. "Not quite."

"The treatment of inmates on death row. Immigration camp conditions. Immigration camps in general. Migrant worker laws. The wage gap. The treatment of minority groups. Detainment of activists. Something called a pink tax?"

Hmm. I leaned toward him, trying to see if he had

a list somewhere he was reading off of. "Is everything on your list protesting?"

"Yes."

"Then you're missing one. I was arrested in Mexico for drug trafficking a few years ago."

Detective Price paused.

Ha! I bet he liked to pretend nothing ever surprised him, but the twitch beside his eye said he wasn't as under control as he thought.

I waited for what felt like ages, until Detective What-Are-You-Talking-About took a breath to say something, then I admitted, "I was innocent that time. They let me out in a day or two. Or was it a week or two? Time's kinda fuzzy."

His eyes widened slightly, but his big tell was the way his face changed color. It wasn't red, exactly, but his skin definitely had a ruddy tint to it that hadn't been there before.

I tried to hide my smile. "I can't really recommend the Mexican jail. There were bedbugs."

Xavier gagged.

Oops. I was having so much fun teasing the detective—no, I'm not saying I made up the arrest down south, because it did happen—that I'd almost forgotten anyone else was there.

That was probably the kind of thing I shouldn't let happen again.

I resettled my glasses as I glanced at Mairi. She didn't look phased. In fact, she didn't look like she'd moved at all.

"You spent anywhere from a day to a couple of

weeks in a jail in Mexico." The detective's hands were too still.

"Uh-huh?" What did he expect me to say?

No, honestly, I'm asking. Because I had no idea what would help the guy's face go back to normal.

And was that a growl?

"I'm okay, really," I hurried to reassure him. "The officers were nice to me."

He said something under his breath, but as close to him as I was, I couldn't make it out. That was some talent he had with his mumbling, because I've gotten pretty good at catching at least bits and pieces of that kind of thing.

Detective Needs-A-Chill-Pill straightened. "Someone left a message with Detective Watson for me to meet you here this afternoon."

"That was me." Mairi piped up. She took a step forward. "Octavia won't use the phone."

Detective Price's face didn't change, but suddenly I was sure he was laughing at me. Deep inside, where he might not even have been aware of it. He tilted his head toward Mairi. "Thank you for doing the dangerous work."

I narrowed my eyes as his twinkled. Obviously his laughter wasn't as deep down as I'd suspected.

A part of me thought I should be annoyed or embarrassed. Instead, laughter bubbled up, spilling out in uncontrollable waves until I lost control and sank to the floor. When my eyes focused again, three faces stared down at me.

Giggles threatened to overtake me again. I bit the inside of my cheek as I worked for control.

From the looks on the faces above me, it obviously wasn't funny to anyone else.

"Is she always like this?" Detective What's-So-Funny asked.

"Unusual?" Mairi asked. "Yes."

At the same time, Xavier hmm'd. "Maybe not always."

I rolled my eyes as I pushed to my feet. "Life's more fun if you actually live it."

"I'm sure the detective knows how to live," Xavier offered, leaning a little too close to the detective.

Detective Price ignored him and met my gaze. "You haven't explained why you needed to see me. Why don't we go outside where we can speak privately?"

It might have been phrased as a question, but experience told me we were going outside whether I wanted to or not. I looked from Xavier to Mairi.

"Go," Mairi reached for me as if she could propel me right through the display case.

"I shouldn't." I was totally going. "What if a customer needs to talk to me?"

"We have things covered." Mairi turned to Xavier. "Right?"

Xavier's shoulders drooped, but he nodded as he gave me a look that made it clear he wanted to hear all the gossip when I got back.

Detective Impatient went to hold the door open.

Pretending to drag my feet, I circled around and

joined him. "I shouldn't be long," I said as I passed Mairi.

"Don't rush on our account," Xavier said. He gave me an exaggerated wink. "I'm sure the good detective would be happy for your insight on things."

Detective Price just held the door a little wider.

Taking the cue, I ignored Xavier's comment and stepped outside.

The detective led me down the path to a bench. We sat, but he didn't say anything until the group of high school-aged students from the music camp down the road passed us by on their way to the concert hall.

I'd forgotten about the resident string quartet's afternoon performance. Back before Ludwig's death had derailed the summer, I'd planned to attend the concert myself. Shostakovich's Quartet No. 8 was a favorite of mine.

Detective Price cleared his throat to get my attention. "I thought you owned the shop, but those two were perfectly comfortable ordering you around."

"They do that." I shrugged. It didn't bother me, and there wasn't really anything I could do to change their behavior even if it did. Well, I suppose I could fire them, but then I'd have to train someone new, and that was a lot of trouble to go to just because my employees were a little more invested in the shop than the detective thought they needed to be. "I don't mind. They're better at business than I am."

He gave me a strange look. "Then why do you own the place?"

"I have to do something. This works for summer." And it didn't tie me down for the rest of the year.

"Just the summer?" Detective Price's eyes went all squinty as he tried not to show he was laughing at me again.

"Aerie Pines is only open in the summer," I reminded him. "I live a simple life, detective. I work the shop in the summer—when Mairi and Xavier let me. The rest of the year, I go wherever the road takes me. If I need more money, I get a temporary job. It works for me."

He stared. "You make no sense to me."

You'd be surprised how often I got that reaction. Or maybe you wouldn't, I don't know. I can't read your mind, can I?

I decided to get to the point. "Last night I went to the party the symphony members have after the season's opening concert."

Detective Price's gaze sharpened, but he waited for another group of students to pass. "Go on."

"Ludwig's murder was the only thing people could talk about." I paused to watch a hawk soaring over the trees.

"Who said it was murder?"

I laughed and turned back to Detective I-Haven't-Told-You-That. "If it wasn't, you wouldn't be investigating."

"We won't know anything for certain until we get the autopsy report back. For now, we're treating this as a suspicious death." Suddenly his rigidness disappeared. "Just between us, I believe it was murder. I'm only telling you so you'll take extra precautions. Don't go anywhere alone, Octavia, and stay as far from the investigation as you can."

Wow. I didn't expect that. For him to act friendly, I mean. Of course I expected him to tell me to stay out of things.

And I really had no intention of trampling on his investigation—or putting myself in danger—so there was nothing for him to worry about. "I didn't ask any questions. I'm leaving that to you. But I did hear some things I thought you should know."

His expression made my stomach flutter.

I pushed my hand against my belly and told it to mellow out. "Ludwig was having some kind of problem with the housing office. There was a big argument or something. Oh! I wonder if it's because he was going to bring his kids up. Maybe there's a rule against that?"

"Did Mr. Baylor tell you they'd be staying with him?"

"What? No. Cora, Ludwig's ex-wife, told me that this morning."

His expression went blank, and suddenly he was back to being a *detective* instead of the guy who did weird things to my insides. "The woman in your shop said you don't use the phone."

"I don't. I drove to the valley to see her."

Detective I-Don't-Like-This worked his jaw. "Why?"

I stuck my tongue out at him. "I have every right to visit my friend."

His eyes narrowed.

"Look, since they were divorced I didn't know if anyone would have told her what happened to Ludwig. I thought it would be better for her to hear it from someone she knew than to find out through word of mouth or on the news." I waited for that to make an impression on him.

No luck.

Man, this guy was hard to please. Not that I was trying to please him, but come on. "Anyway, she said Ludwig had promised the kids they could come stay with him. But Cora probably already told you that."

Even though Cora hadn't said it was a secret, I couldn't help feeling I was letting her down by sharing what she'd said. But this seemed like the kind of thing the detective should know.

"Did you hear any other gossip?"

He did not just relegate my information to gossip.

Cop or no cop, he didn't scare me. I crossed my arms. Fine, maybe it was gossip, but still. It was useful gossip. Gossip that might give him a lead he didn't already have.

Detective My-Information-Is-Better-Than-Yours waited.

I pulled a face at him.

He breathed loudly.

As much as I hate to admit it, I caved. "Tatiana

didn't have to kill Ludwig to get rid of him. She was supposed to meet with the symphony board."

I spilled all the information she'd shared with me, as well as the information about contract renewal auditions Xavier had been asking about.

Detective Price might have thought I was spouting gossip, but he at least paid attention. "So he might have been out of a job soon anyway."

I nodded. There were more details to the situation, but that was the gist of it. "So do we talk to Tatiana first, or the housing office?"

Nine

"I TALK TO THESE PEOPLE." Detective Price pointed to himself, then turned his finger toward me. "You go back to whatever it is you do in a violin shop."

Rude. It wasn't as if I was trying to go with him. I just wanted to know what the next step was and the we had slipped out. "Excuse me?"

"You don't trust me. Knowing your history with the law I suppose it's only natural." He sat up taller as if he was trying to intimidate me into trusting him.

Well, Detective You're-Just-A-Common-Criminal had better think again. I don't intimidate easily.

Besides, who in their right mind would trust someone who always pulled rank? I decided to turn the conversation on him. "Whatever I do in a violin shop? You must not be a very good detective if you can't even figure that out."

His brows drew together and he gave his head a little shake. "You sell violins?"

"And violas, and cellos." Okay, so we rarely sold instruments. Not my fault, I promise. The musicians at the nearby summer programs already had instruments, and obviously the symphony members did, too. And really, finding the right instrument is a long process where you compare pretty much everything in your price range from every shop you can drive to. For something really special—with the appropriately high price tag to make shipping it unreasonable—you might fly across the country to try it out. "We also do repairs, and soundpost adjustments, and we have all the accessories string musicians need."

"So your shop is busy."

"Sure?"

Now, I'm not saying the shop is busy enough Xavier and Mairi couldn't handle it on their own. This was just the beginning of the season. Things would pick up in a week or two, and get really busy mid-summer, but even then my staff could handle it without me. As they liked to remind me.

Detective Something-Up-His-Sleeve smiled.

Why did he have to have such a good smile?

"Then I'd suggest you focus on keeping the shop busy instead of putting yourself in the middle of my investigation."

"I'm a multitasker." I tried to wait him out, I really did, but the man had the patience of someone teaching a three-year-old to play the violin. I grabbed my hair and tossed it behind my shoulder.

"I wanted to know what the next steps were, not to walk them myself."

He turned and met my gaze head-on.

My head began to swim.

No. No. I wasn't going to do the fainting damsel thing. I wasn't that woman.

Refusing to break the silence this time, I rolled the hem of my skirt in my fingers, focusing on the bumpiness of the serged edge.

When he spoke, his voice was rough. "If I tell you what I plan to do, you'll stay safely in your shop?"

I wasn't going to promise to stay in the shop. How could I? No one really needed me there. Besides, I had to go home at night. Instead of giving him an actual answer, I just smiled.

Detective Price pinched the bridge of his nose, then finally nodded. "I'll see what I can find out at the housing office, as well as talk to this violinist of yours."

Well, if he was going to take my smile as agreement, I wasn't going to tell him it wasn't. Besides, he didn't tell me anything I hadn't already deduced. "That's all?"

"I didn't have to tell you that much," Detective High-And-Mighty grumbled. Then, looking almost surprised that the words were coming out, he went on. "I'm waiting on reports and test results. It'll probably be a few days before those come in. Maybe longer, depending on the lab's backlog. Until then I'll keep asking questions. This isn't glamorous work, Ms. Fields. There are rules and procedures—and a lot of dead ends."

I played his game and waited to see what else he'd say, but he went quiet. When the silence had stretched almost to the point where a normal person might consider it uncomfortable, I decided to see if his sharing mood might reach as far as giving me actual information. "You went to see Cora. Is that normal, to visit a victim's ex-wife? Or ex-husband. Ex-spouse."

Piper chose that moment to walk out of the next building over. There was nothing scheduled in the auditorium, but she liked to check out all the nooks and crannies. That was fine by me—as long as she didn't find another body stuffed in one.

My friend waved at me and started over. Then she noticed who was sitting beside me and her eyes widened. She did a quick about-face and went back inside.

"It depends," Detective Selective-Vision answered my question while pretending he hadn't noticed Piper's odd reaction to seeing him. "In this case it was prudent. There are children involved. Also, I needed to see her reaction to the news."

Oh, right. I hadn't thought about the kids being next-of-kin. I'd been thinking of adults. "What about her reaction?"

The corners of his eyes tightened. He must not have meant to let that slip.

I sat forward. "Did she pass your test?"

"No comment."

"She was pretty upset when I stopped by." I twisted my lips to the side and pretended to think. "If she'd wanted to hurt him, she's had years. Besides, she was miles and miles away."

Detective Price hesitated. His eyes cleared, some decision made. "The victim didn't change his will after the divorce. By design, or because he hadn't taken the time, I don't know. His ex-wife inherited everything."

"If Ludwig wanted to cut her out, he'd have done it the second the divorce was final. He never put off being vindictive."

"That fits the picture I'm getting of him." He started to say something else, then changed his mind and pushed to his feet. "Thank you for the information. Try not to learn anything else, okay?"

Something inside ached at the idea of him walking off. My curiosity, obviously. I didn't really expect him to answer—he'd already given me more than I had any right to expect—but I had to ask. "Where are you going?"

He looked at the sky. "To find the housing office."

I craned my neck to see what had caught his eye, but the sky was clear. Maybe he was greeting the sun. Odd that he waited until he was leaving, but better late than never. "I could show you where it is."

"That's not a good idea."

"Why, because you think I'm going to follow you in and eavesdrop?" I crossed my eyes and stuck my tongue out at him again.

He laughed and offered me his elbow. "Fine. Guide me, O Wise One."

I tucked my arm through his, trying not to notice the muscles rippling under my fingers.

Obviously I failed. I mean, it's not like I was trying all that hard.

If Detective Price offers you his arm and you manage not to notice how strong he is, you can judge me. Until then, just let me enjoy it. Okay?

"No shoes again?"

That's right. While I was noticing him, he was noticing me. Well, my bare feet.

Maybe he hadn't believed me when I told him I owned shoes.

I kicked my foot up and wiggled my toes in answer.

"Aren't you worried about splinters? Or what about ticks?" His voice was full of practiced concern.

"Nope. If I'm meant to pick up anything like that, I will. Wearing shoes won't change that, so I might as well be comfortable." I pointed toward a set of five buildings with my free hand. "We're going in that first building in the back."

The housing office was tucked inside a building that was also home to building maintenance and some other "unimportant" departments. They were the necessary people who were mostly ignored despite the fact that they were the ones who kept the whole place going.

Life's weird that way.

We stepped into a bare hallway. I turned us the right direction and stopped outside an unmarked door. "This is it."

Detective Price looked up and down the hallway. "Almost feels like they don't want to be found."

"Outside of those who already know where it is, very few people need to find it." I released his elbow and stepped back.

"Thank you for getting me here." He seemed to grow as his posture firmed, somehow getting both taller and wider. "You can go back to your shop."

"Sure." I leaned on the wall across from the door. I totally wanted to see the housing team's reaction when this guy walked in. They weren't used to getting visitors beyond people picking up or dropping off keys, or letting them know there was a problem with their apartment.

Or their room, if they were staying in the Lodge.

Or their cabin, if they were a VIP.

"I mean it, Ms. Fields. Go play with your violins and forget there's an investigation going on. I don't want to see you here when I come out." He opened the door and stepped through. As the door closer did its job, Detective Orders-People-Around gave me a pointed look over his shoulder.

I peeled myself off the wall. He could keep me out of there, but he couldn't send me back to the shop like a kid being sent to their room for not practicing. How many times did I need to tell him

I wasn't trying to intrude into his investigation? I just wanted the whole thing to be over so life could go back to normal.

The shop could very well do without me, but there wasn't a reason for me to stay, so I started down the hall.

After a few steps, I noticed a door that hadn't been there the last time I'd wandered through the building. Curious, I turned the doorknob and peeked inside to find a small, unfinished room, hardly more than a closet. A custodial cart and a set of shelves took up most of the space, but that wasn't what caught my attention.

There was a grille in the wall.

Was it for air flow? Or just to cover a part of the wall they hadn't gotten to yet? I had no idea.

What I did know was that the voice coming through it belonged to Detective Go-Away.

I debated for all of two seconds, then stepped into the room and closed the door.

Yes, he told me to leave. No, the investigation wasn't any of my business. But I was curious.

I bet you would have stayed, too.

Paying attention to the contents of the closet so I wouldn't bump into anything and give myself away, I sat cross-legged on the floor.

Through the horizontal slats of the grille, I watched Detective Price amble around the room. He might look relaxed and at ease, but even without a clear view I could make out the careful set of those broad shoulders. And that wasn't his devastating smile, more of just a slightly upturned mouth that made him look slightly more approachable than he'd been the first time I saw him.

So, approachable like a hungry bear, or like a violinist trying to hit the double stops of Bach's Partita in D minor when their instrument hasn't been tuned in a week.

Where was everyone else? He'd just been talking to someone, but he appeared to be alone—as far as I could see, anyway.

I leaned closer to the grille.

Two women came out of the inner office.

A tall woman with practical short hair and a brisk step took charge. "What can we do for you?"

"You're the office manager?" Detective Price asked.

"As much as there is one. We split responsibilities equally around here."

I was so busy trying not to snort—as much as there is one—that I almost missed the other woman bobbing her head in agreement.

Detective Price pulled out his phone to take notes. Unless he was checking his texts or emails or whatever else people do with the devices in their hands. "I'm Detective Price."

It didn't take long for the office manager to get tired of the expectant quiet. "Vanessa Chambers. And this is Tammy Spencer. Are you sure you're in the right place? This is the housing office."

"I'm sure you've heard there was a death at the

amphitheater. A man by the name of Ludwig Baylor." The words felt like a warning despite the fact that Detective Price spoke them in a matter-of-fact way.

Vanessa gave a short laugh. "Everyone's heard about it. The thing about a place like Aerie Pines, Detective, is that the proximity of everyone living on-site means there are very few secrets."

Oh, there were plenty of secrets. Some were just kept better than others.

If you wanted to keep something secret around here, there were certain people you had to either keep the information away from, or have a good enough friendship with them that they'd be willing to hold their tongue.

Like Piper and Xavier. They loved to know everything that was going on, but if one of their friends confided in them, there was no way they'd spill the information to the other gossips.

Another way to keep a secret was to just not talk about something at all. I mean, no one around here had a clue why Morton and I had broken up, even if his backing out of conducting a concert had basically announced that the relationship was over.

And no, I'm not about to tell you that. Didn't I just say you don't tell anyone something if it's a secret?

Okay, so it's not really a secret, but Piper should hear about it first. *She is* my best friend.

"You're right about that." Detective Price's comment brought me back to the conversation.

"Secrets have a way of coming to light, especially during an investigation. I've been told Mr. Baylor was upset when he left your office."

The ladies glanced at each other.

"Why don't you tell me about it." There was the detective's *let's pretend you have a choice in the matter even though we both know better* voice.

"What have you heard?" Vanessa countered.

Detective Price stayed so quiet I found myself holding my breath so the sound of it wouldn't get me caught.

Tammy made a small sound. "Mr. Baylor said his apartment was too small. He thought his importance in the symphony meant he should have something better. He wouldn't even move into the apartment."

"He should have had a room in the Lodge," Vanessa cut in. "The only reason he had an apartment was because the symphony board insisted. Something about it being in his contract."

Vanessa made it sound like being in the Lodge was a bad thing, but a lot of people chose it. Sure, you only had the one room—fine, they got their own bathroom, too—but the dining room took care of all their meals, and they had easy access to the Lodge's entertainment rooms.

"Go on."

"I told him I couldn't change the assignments, even if I wanted to," Tammy said. "The cabins were already taken."

I hadn't heard who was staying in the large

cabins this year. They really were large enough to house a team of people. Sometimes a composer was invited to be a summer resident. Sometimes they were kept for visiting conductors, or members of the Aerie Peaks Symphony Board. Last summer a movie star and their entourage spent a month in one.

"A single man doesn't need the two bedroom apartment he was assigned," Vanessa insisted. "He had no business asking for a cabin."

Detective Price shifted his weight, and the women froze. "How do you decide who stays where?"

"Everyone gets something, their contracts say so. They're invited to make requests for where they want to be." Vanessa started counting on her fingers. "Musicians who bring a spouse or family have priority on apartments. People who are alone or don't want to cook are in the Lodge. People we've had trouble with in the past are trickier. They have to go where previous years' experiences won't be repeated. VIPs are sometimes put in the hotel, especially if they're only here for a week or two. And symphony members never get the cabins."

"And that's what caused the problem with the victim?" Detective Price asked.

There was no answer.

What were they doing? I leaned forward until my face was almost pressed against the grille.

They were all just standing there.

Finally, Vanessa nodded. "He never said why he

wanted the cabin, but he came back a dozen times, angrier each visit. He threatened to have us fired, as if that man had any say in who works here."

Detective Price waited another minute, then reached into his pocket and pulled out a card. "If you think of anything else, you can reach me at this number."

I started to lean away from the grill as he turned. His eyes paused on the grille.

Uh-oh. Had he seen the movement?

He left the office, and I waited for the door to my hiding place to open.

It didn't.

I was trying to decide if that meant I was safe, when Vanessa's voice shot through the quiet Detective Price had left in his wake. "You did well."

"Well." Through the grill I saw Tammy throw the card on a desk. It was a good thing it was just paper. If it had been something heavy, that kind of force would have dented the desk. "It's not like I was going to risk my job by telling the detective you threatened to kill Ludwig Baylor if he dared to come back here. I wish you hadn't said that right before he was found murdered."

Ten

My viola woke up as I tuned it, sending vibrations rippling into my shoulder. Some musicians relied only on their ears to tell them if something was in tune, not just when tuning but when playing. But the instrument was a living thing. I'd always found the vibrations of the wood told me more than my ears.

I let my fingers fall onto the string, noodling as my thoughts wandered.

How could I tell Detective Price what I'd overheard after he left without admitting I'd defied him by eavesdropping on his interview with the ladies at the housing office?

I could tell him I'd heard a rumor that Vanessa had threatened Ludwig, but if he wanted to know who told me, I wouldn't have an answer. Unless I lied.

Which was a valid option, I'll have you know. Even if I don't normally see any reason to lie—I don't normally mind owning my mistakes—it was always something I could fall back on. But it would be easier if I didn't have to.

Soon my noodling gave way to music any violist would recognize. The piece wasn't as technically challenging as many that I loved, but the melodies of *Harold in Italy* spoke to the wanderlust that lived in my soul. Berlioz painted such vistas with the notes that playing them always left me itching to go out and find places that breathed the same feelings.

I gripped the string with my bow, pulling out a richer tone, letting the music transport me. Everything disappeared—the questions, the shop's instrument room, even the memory of Ludwig's body sprawled on the floor.

The only thing that existed was the music, and my connection to it. My mind inserted the orchestra part, filling out and supporting the notes I played.

When the last of the music settled, my mind was calm.

"You should play more often." Piper leaned against the door, looking like she'd been there for ages. "I think people have forgotten you're an actual musician."

I cradled my viola, then reached for a cloth to wipe away the rosin dust. "I play for myself, not for them."

"Of course you do. You've never needed accolades or attention, but it wouldn't hurt to let other people listen."

Having an audience came with unspoken rules. They liked to know what you were going to perform, for one thing. For another, they wanted you to look the part, which I never had. And then you had to stick around afterward so they could tell you how much they enjoyed it, or that it touched them.

The best was when they said *"I've never heard it played like that before."* That's what you say to someone when you think their performance was lacking but don't necessarily want them to realize it. You're supposed to smile and thank them, but on rare occasions it can be fun to turn it on them and ask what in particular they found unusual.

They either stumble and stammer to find something to say that you won't recognize as an insult, or they make up something that's obviously a lie, or they shut down and leave.

I mean, you have to be selective in whose nose you tweak like that, but we musicians are a strange lot. Well, some of us are.

Fine. Maybe it's just me.

Loosening my bow, I put it away, then nestled my viola in and shut the case. "Frenzy and Buttercup like to listen. Maybe I should give them a concert tonight."

"The squirrel you let run around your home?"

"And the doe. Or haven't I told you about Buttercup yet? She stays outside." I pretended not to see the look on Piper's face. "Probably a good thing. There just isn't a lot of room inside for an animal that size."

Piper started to say something, then shook her head.

Then her eyes took on a dreamy quality and she pressed her hands over her heart. "I bet Detective Price wouldn't mind being your audience."

I rolled my eyes. Piper was in love with love and liked to see it everywhere. She'd probably be pushing me at Detective Broad-Shoulders even if Morton's cancellation hadn't announced we weren't together anymore. "The detective is busy. He's only here because of Ludwig."

"He can't work all the time." She lowered herself into an armchair and crossed her legs. Her eyelashes did their fluttering thing. "What did he want with you before?"

"I was telling him some of the gossip I've picked up that might help with his investigation."

"He offered you his arm." Piper's eyelashes went crazy.

"So?"

"A man like that doesn't let people get close when he's working a case. This man invited you to touch him." If Piper smiled any bigger she'd look like that freaky cat from the animated movie my parents made me watch when I was young. "He let his guard down with you. He wanted you in his space, Octavia."

Normally it was easy to take Piper's quirks in stride, but something about her turning that focus on the detective felt out of place. "You do know you're not some old-timey matchmaker, right? No one's going to burst into song asking you to find them a find."

Piper tossed her head. "If there was ever a man who didn't need help finding his match, it's Detective Price."

"Exactly." He was the kind of man who had to beg women to leave him alone. No wonder he had a job where he carried a gun. The only thing I didn't understand was why Piper hadn't tried to flirt with him during her questioning.

I opened the door and stepped into the main part of the shop. The quartet concert must have ended. The shop was full of teenagers. I moved behind the counter and jumped in to help a girl who needed a new rubber tip for the foot of her shoulder rest so the metal wouldn't scratch her violin.

Piper finger waved high above her head as she sashayed out the door.

It wasn't long before the rush died down. I tried to straighten the disarray left behind, but the horror in Xavier's eyes stopped me from re-arranging things.

Mairi, of course, was trying to remove every fingerprint from the glass.

I went into the office, instead.

The room was big enough we could have staff meetings if we needed to, with a large desk at the far end and a small sofa next to it. I pulled out the wheeled desk chair and sat down, staring at the large safe where Ludwig's violin was tucked away.

Ludwig might have been a jerk sometimes—most of the time—but he deserved justice. If Vanessa had really threatened him, Detective Price should talk to her again. Even if it meant admitting I'd spied on their conversation.

I looked around the desk for his card, but came up emptyhanded. Mairi had probably stashed it somewhere "safe" after she'd made the call this morning. I double checked the drawers, then left the office. "Will one of you call the detective for me?"

"Again?" Mairi asked. "I thought he was just here."

"You don't want to look desperate," Xavier added. He leaned on the counter, but when Mairi glared at him he straightened and grabbed a cloth to remove any marks he might have left behind. "Is it true Morton isn't coming this summer because the two of you broke up? Is that why you're so interested in the detective?"

Breathe in. Breathe out. It didn't matter if they thought I was angling to see the detective about something other than Ludwig's death. "I'm not interested in Detective Price, I just have to tell him something. And I don't know why Morton isn't coming, but yes, we broke up."

They were both talking at me, but their words bounced off without making any sense. I started toward the door. The detective was going to talk to Tatiana. Maybe he was still at Aerie Pines.

I grabbed my bike and rode down to the parking lot. There were no police cars, but I wasn't sure if the detective drove one of those, or if he had one of those black unmarked bigger vehicles with dark windows the government thought people wouldn't notice. Unfortunately, I didn't see any of those, either. Not sure what else to do, I turned around. I'd just have to keep an eye out. He'd come back eventually.

On my way back to the shop I had to pass the Aerie Pines offices. I braked and pulled to the side of the path.

I was right here. What would it hurt for me to go in and talk to the women?

Nothing, that's what. It would be easy to nose around a little. If they said anything about this threat, I could pass the information on to Detective Stay-Out-Of-It.

And if not, well, he didn't ever need to find out.

I went around to the back building. Since there were no bike racks, I leaned Clover against the wall and headed in. The housing office door stood open, so I didn't knock. Instead, I walked right into a complaint.

"The faucet is backwards. Hot water comes out when you turn on the cold." A man I vaguely recognized as a trumpeter was—not yelling, exactly, but speaking aggressively.

Vanessa didn't look the least bit cowed. "Just

turn it to hot if you want cold. See? It works just fine."

"I just need someone to fix it."

"Don't be unreasonable. You have water, don't you?" She shooed him away. "I don't have time for made-up problems."

He left, but he didn't look happy about it.

I made a mental note to ask Hector if he knew someone in maintenance who might be willing to slip in and fix the faucet without letting Vanessa find out about it.

"And what's your problem?" Vanessa turned a harried expression my way. "Don't you own the violin shop? I didn't know you were staying here. No, you're not on my list. I didn't assign you anything."

"Oh, I'm not looking for a place to stay. It's just—I'm the one who found Ludwig's body, and I'm trying to make sense of it." Honesty might be the best policy, but this seemed like a situation where it could use a little help. I crossed my toes for good measure. Vanessa could see my fingers. "I know he came to the office, and I hoped maybe you could tell me something that would help. Anything."

Tammy left a desk in the corner where I hadn't noticed her.

Now that I was getting a better look at her, I wasn't surprised she'd blended into the background. Her wispy hair was the same almost-white blonde as the walls, and her too-big-for-her shirt was only a shade darker.

"I spoke with him." Tammy's voice pulled me away from noticing how pale she was. "You think the guy who just left was unreasonable? Mr. Baylor makes that guy look like a pussycat."

I almost told her I didn't think the trumpeter seemed unreasonable, but stopped myself. If I wanted to get anything out of these ladies, it would be better if I stayed on their good side.

"I'd heard he had an argument." This was feeling less and less like a good idea, but the words wouldn't stop spilling out of my mouth. "Someone said he'd been threatened."

Vanessa slapped her hand on her thigh. "Why do people care? That man was horrible."

"He was. Sometimes, anyway. Usually?" What percentage of the time was considered sometimes, and what was usually?

"I didn't mean anything by it." Vanessa exploded. "I was angry. He wouldn't leave me alone. How was I supposed to know he was going to get himself killed?"

Tammy glanced back and forth between us, a crease between her brows.

The energy in the room was so dark I expected to see everything outlined in black. "What did you say?"

Vanessa smashed her lips together.

"She told him—" Tammy started.

Vanessa glared at her.

"She told him if he came back again, she'd kill him." She turned to Vanessa. "I didn't tell the detective, but someone was bound to find out. You know he left here ready to tell anyone he saw. I don't want to lose my job over it, but I can't lie for you."

Vanessa turned on me. "I didn't mean it. It's just something you say when you're angry."

I nodded as if I understood why someone would invite that kind of harm and negativity into their body. Based on the venom in her voice now, I wondered just how angry Vanessa had been when it happened.

Angry enough to do something to make sure Ludwig would stay away for good?

Eleven

THE NEXT MORNING, AFTER A quiet night sitting beside the open flames of the fire pit by my gypsy caravan, enjoying the fresh air and making little piles of nuts for Frenzy, I pedaled Clover back to Aerie Pines.

The music camps had been invited to observe the symphony's morning rehearsal, which meant the students would be stopping by the shop in droves before and after, and maybe during the break. That meant Mairi and Xavier would be happy to see me, which was always nice.

I let myself into the shop. Music came from the workshop, so I stuck my head through the door to say good morning.

Eli looked over from the bow he was straightening. "Did the woman with the rehair ever come in for the bow after she wasn't there to meet you?"

"Tatiana stopped in yesterday. Why, was there a problem with it?"

He laughed. "No, nothing like that. I was just

going to take a closer look if it was still here. Maybe take some pictures. It was a nice bow."

Of course it was. Tatiana took her craft seriously. I didn't know where she'd gotten the bow, but the woman made sure she had the best tools she could afford.

I turned to Jamie. He had an unfinished violin top on the bench in front of him. A set of finger planes stood in a row within easy reach, but there were no wood shavings in sight. He was just looking at the wood.

I slipped out of the workshop without saying anything to him. I wasn't about to interrupt his morning ritual. Well, it wasn't just a morning ritual. He did the same thing every time he switched between projects.

After making sure Ludwig's Gagliano was still safe in the safe—sure, only Detective Price and I knew the current combination for it, but I wasn't taking any chances—I swept the floor of the shop and straightened the displays, careful not to mess up the organization system that didn't have to make sense to me.

When Mairi and Xavier came in together, the first thing they did was check to make sure I hadn't moved anything around.

"It looks okay," Mairi said. Then she held out the stack of mail. "I stopped and grabbed this."

"Is there anything that isn't an ad?" Distributing companies could save a lot of trees if they'd stop trying to get me to buy from them. I already had companies I liked working with.

And we needed those trees.

Maybe I should spearhead a protest. We could make signs that said Oxygen doesn't just happen, it grows on trees and Save Mother Earth—Adopt a forest!

I thought through the protests I'd been to, trying to decide which location would be best for this kind of topic.

"Here's a new cello case company. This place has a special on strings. Here's a sheet music catalog." Mairi counted things off as she flipped through the stack. Then she stopped and pushed a letter into my hands. "I don't know what this one is, but it's addressed to you."

"You can recycle the rest." I ripped open the envelope and pulled out a single sheet of paper. It took a minute for the words to sink in.

Stop your investigation.

Ludwig got what he deserved.

I resettled my glasses and read the note again. Was this a threat? I didn't want to believe it was, but I wasn't going to take any chances. "Mairi, call Detective Price."

"I know I work for you, but I'm not your secretary." She read the note over my shoulder. "Never mind. I'll get his card."

"What is it?" Xavier reached for the page as Mairi disappeared into the office.

"Don't touch it. The detective might want to see if there are fingerprints." I carefully set the note on the glass that Mairi kept painfully clean.

"Oh." The pitch of Xavier's voice was higher than normal. "I thought you said you weren't investigating. Who have you talked to? What did they say? Can I tell Piper?"

Of course he wanted to gossip about it. "Let's see what Detective Price has to say about it before we make any plans."

Xavier pouted.

I didn't really blame him. Of course the detective was going to tell him not to say anything. People in law enforcement liked to control who knew what. Maybe it helped with solving their cases, or maybe they were just control freaks. Or maybe it was a little bit of both.

Mairi ended the call as she came back. "He's on his way. Do we have a plastic bag big enough to hold that? Something that hasn't been used, so it won't contaminate the evidence."

"Of course we don't." Plastic was another thing that was killing the world. Even protests weren't going to help stop that. Our society was too reliant on the stuff. Hundreds, maybe thousands, of people were doing their best to avoid using plastic, but it was going to take thousands more committing to the cause if we were going to make even a small difference.

"That's what I told him," Mairi said. "He didn't seem impressed."

Yet another reason why the man wasn't my type, even if he was nice to look at.

"He said if we can't find one, to just lock the door and keep people out."

"We're expecting a busy morning," Xavier argued.

"The paper already has my fingerprints on it," I said. "I'll just take it in the office. We can lock that door—does it have a lock?—and keep it safe."

Mairi grabbed my arm before I could pick up the note. "He said not to touch it anymore."

"Okay. Hold on." I went and stuck my head back into the workshop.

Jamie had moved on from staring at the wood to using those tiny finger planes. He didn't look up when I went in.

"Can I borrow your tweezers?" I asked.

Without looking at me, he grabbed them and held them out. "I need them back. Today. This morning. Don't use them for your eyebrows or anything gross."

"Nothing gross," I promised. "Just paper. I'll bring them back in two minutes."

It took several trips, but I got the note and every piece of envelope into the office by tweezing the tiniest edges. I settled them in the middle of the desktop that Mairi quickly wiped down so nothing could transfer and ruin any evidence.

Then I took the tweezers back to Jamie before I could forget.

It wasn't long before the shop opened. Students came in, some just browsing, others hoping we had tourist stuff they could send home to family, but a few were actually there to buy the kind of things we sold.

Xavier rang up a set of strings, while Mairi helped a young woman choose a new mute. I got to help the man with wild hair and hands that couldn't stop moving select a new rock stop. He finally settled on one carved from a pale wood that would attach to his chair.

Things were starting to settle back down by the time Detective Price walked in. He held the door for a frazzled high school girl who'd wanted us to swap out her ebony pegs for an embellished rosewood set but hadn't realized they had to be specially fitted and she'd need to leave her cello with us for a few days.

Detective Price wove his way through the remaining customers until he was standing in front of me. He raised his eyebrows in a silent question.

One that I didn't understand.

Was he asking if I'd found a plastic bag? Which, of course, I hadn't even tried to do. Or was he asking why there were customers in a shop? Or where I'd put the note?

Finally, he used words. "Are you okay?"

I looked down at myself, inspecting my hands and arms for something that was obviously wrong.

"It can be hard to get—" he glanced around to see if anyone was paying attention "—that kind of thing in the mail."

Oh. That was . . . sweet. Not what I expected. "I'm fine. I guess you want to see it?"

"That's why I'm here." He smiled his Detective Devastating smile.

My heart did a little pitter-patter thing. I really needed to focus on my breath work so I could control that better. "It's in the office."

He followed me in, closing the door behind us. The sounds of the shop dropped off sharply.

I pointed to the desk.

Detective Price read the note with a single sweep of his eyes. His jaw hardened. "This came in the mail?"

"Yes."

He was already pulling on a pair of disposable gloves and reaching for the pieces of envelope. "Postmarked late yesterday. Is there a post office nearby, or is the closest one at the base of the canyon?"

I shrugged. "I don't know."

He looked at me.

"What? It's not like I ever mail anything." Summer was the only time I stayed in the same place long enough for mail to catch up with me, but that didn't mean I knew the post office situation for the mountain. On the extremely rare occasion I had to mail something, I just dropped it in one of the big boxes.

"I'll look into it. This was postmarked in a little town just before you hit the canyon, which makes sense if it's the nearest post office. If not, it might mean someone is trying to throw suspicion elsewhere." He took a plastic bag from his pocket and slid the envelope inside. Then he picked up the note. "I thought I told you not to investigate."

I tried to laugh. It sounded like a cross between a choking cat and a hyena. "Who said I'm investigating?"

He waved the note.

Well, I guess that was pretty obvious, wasn't it? "Everyone thinks I'm helping you. No," I hurried on before he could get mad at me, "I didn't tell anyone that. But somehow people got the idea. People I hardly know were coming up to me at the symphony party the other night asking how it was going, or giving me tips because I was helping you. It's not my fault if people don't listen when I tell them this is your thing, not mine."

He slid the paper into the bag with the envelope. "I want a list of everyone you've talked to about this."

"Everyone?" That would include Vanessa Chambers and Tammy Spencer, and I hadn't decided what I thought of that whole situation.

"Everyone."

"I don't know everyone's names," I hedged.

He sighed. "Just do your best."

As I nodded, I wondered how long I could put off making the list. I didn't want anyone thinking I was talking behind their backs.

That was Piper's thing, and everyone knew it.

Detective Price motioned for me to sit on the couch. "You said you spoke with the ex-wife."

"Cora. I already told you about that." I paused as his implication struck me. "You can't think she's really a suspect. She was far away, and she doesn't even have a motive. She'd already divorced him."

"But you spoke with her."

"Fine, I spoke with her." I took a deep breath. Two minutes alone with the man and I was losing all the zen I'd worked to reclaim with my quiet evening alone. "I also spoke with Mairi and Xavier, and Piper, and most of the people at the bonfire, and I talked to the housing office."

"You went to the housing office." The negative vibes suddenly rolling off him made me shiver. "I told you I was handling it."

I grabbed a fistful of hair and tossed it over my shoulder. "Of course you're handling it. Did Vanessa tell you she threatened to kill Ludwig if he went back to bother her again?"

Uh, oh. His face was doing the changing color thing.

I stood back up. Detective Can't-Control-His-Temper wouldn't be the first angry cop who'd towered over me, but I wasn't about to take it sitting down. "Look, it's not a big deal. All I did was tell them I'd heard he was really angry when he left. They filled in the rest."

My attempt at placating him wasn't working.

His face had gone from slightly-mottled to red.

The man seriously needed to mellow out.

I tried again. "It's nothing to worry about."

"Nothing to worry about," Detective Price ground out. "Nothing to worry about. You just went to talk to a murder suspect on your own. I bet you didn't even tell anyone where you were going."

When he put it that way, I guess it did sound a little reckless.

"And now you're receiving threats in the mail," he continued.

"Hey! There was only one threat."

"You are the one person I'm entirely convinced is innocent in this case. Innocent of murder, anyway," he corrected. "I can't hang around waiting to protect you, Octavia. I have my work cut out trying to wrap up this case. I would appreciate it if you could manage not to become any more of a victim while I find the right person to arrest."

"I'm not a victim."

He waved the plastic-encased threat under my nose.

"Okay, but it's only a tiny thing. Just one little letter." If I could make him feel better about the situation maybe I wouldn't have to worry about it, either. "Wait. If I'm innocent of murder, does that mean . . . it was definitely murder? You're not looking at it as an accident anymore?"

I shivered. Those eyes burning into mine were way too intense. "The back of his head was crushed, and the statue that had blood residue on its base was sitting where I'm told it belonged. Even if the victim had lost his balance and smacked his own head into it, it didn't put itself back on the pedestal six feet away from him."

The image I'd been trying not to see jumped to the front of my mind. There was Ludwig, sprawled on the floor. And there was the only statue nearby—a bust of Mozart.

"I won't consider this threat a prank. That would put you at even greater risk," he said. "Somehow, whether it's because you spoke with them or because people have assumed you're helping solve this case, you're on the killer's radar. I refuse to let you be their next victim."

Twelve

"YOU'LL NEVER GUESS WHAT I heard while you were out," Xavier said.

After Detective Price's news that there was indeed a murderer hanging around, I'd thought about going home for the rest of the day. Instead, I'd settled for taking a long lunch to walk through the woods and get in some quality earthing.

"Let her get inside first." For once, Mairi wasn't polishing the glass. She was busy sorting through receipts instead.

"She's all the way through the door and everything." He turned back to me and pumped his hands along with each of his next words. "There is *good* gossip."

I didn't have the heart to tell him I didn't care. "What?"

"Remember you said Tatiana had made plans to meet with the symphony board?"

"Sure." Since I was the one who'd spoken with her, it was likely Xavier would forget before I did.

Scratch that. Xavier remembered gossip better even than Piper.

Or did he just remember everything better than I did? I mean, the fact that Tatiana had an appointment with the board wasn't exactly gossip. Was it weird that he was remembering some random person's calendar appointments?

Xavier was squirming around like a violinist who hadn't learned to move with the music but wanted to look like he had. "She already met with them. That's why she wasn't there to pick up her bow."

"She was with the board when Ludwig died?" I asked. I'd been so sure she was a valid suspect.

If Tatiana was with the entire board at the time, what we had was a valid alibi.

I didn't want to believe it.

No, it wasn't because I didn't like her. Didn't I already say she could be perfectly nice to other people? I thought she was a suspect because she was supposed to be in the greenroom at the time Ludwig was killed.

Killed.

The high I'd worked so hard to ride during lunch abruptly flattened out.

And Detective Takes-His-Job-Seriously said I was the only one not on his suspect list. Surely he'd spoken with Tatiana by now. If she'd had that kind of an alibi he would have already confirmed her innocence.

Mairi opened the cash register and tucked the

receipts back in their place. "Piper didn't say when the meeting was."

"This came from Piper?"

Xavier pouted. "Fine, it came from Piper. And she didn't say anything more than I already told you."

I'd just have to talk to her myself. "Are you okay if I'm gone for a while?"

Without waiting for an answer, I turned and went back outside and headed toward the turnoff that went up to the main housing area.

A woman fell into step beside me. "Ms. Fields."

"Detective Watson. What are you doing here? Not that you aren't welcome, of course. I'm just surprised. I knew Detective Price was here this morning, but he didn't say anyone else would be around and . . ." I trailed off as her expression hardened.

How did she do that? Were there special muscles you learned to use in police school? I couldn't quite picture a room full of soon-to-be cops looking into a mirror while flexing facial muscles.

"After you received the threat this morning, Detective Price and the rest of the team decided we needed to keep an eye on you. For your own protection." She added the last sentence as an afterthought.

"Like a bodyguard?"

Detective Watson hesitated. "Something like that."

That hesitation told me everything I needed to know. She wasn't a bodyguard, she was supposed to keep me from causing trouble.

I'd never had a police tail before. I wasn't sure I was going to like it. For one thing, it meant I wouldn't be able to ask Piper about the board meeting without the detectives knowing about it before the conversation had even ended.

"You aren't worried that having people see you with me will convince them I'm working with you?" I could just picture the color Detective Price's face would turn.

"I'm undercover." She gestured to her clothes. Instead of a suit like she'd worn the other day, Detective Watson wore dark jeans and a silk blouse.

"You look nice," I said. She still looked like a cop. "You might be a little bit overdressed."

"It's jeans," she said.

The jeans were fine. The blouse was fine. But something about the way she combined them felt fancy.

Or maybe it's just that she made me feel shabby.

Which was stupid. So I was wearing some of my favorite thrift store finds. So what? Giving clothes a second life was the responsible thing to do. It kept them out of the landfill.

And why on earth did I care if the woman thought I was shabby? I'd never thought twice about my eclectic style before these detectives marched into my life.

Ugh, no. I wasn't going to let them steal my

happiness. As soon as they finished their work here, I'd never see them again. "As long as you're comfortable."

Detective Watson started walking in the direction I'd been going.

I kept pace with her. "I'm sure you have better things to do than keep me company. It's okay. I can take care of myself."

She surprised me by laughing. "No offense, but I'm not sure you can."

"You don't even know me," I pointed out. Sure, I was used to people making snap judgments about me, but somehow I hadn't expected Detective Watson to make one.

You think I'm naive for thinking she might at least want to know some things about me before deciding something like that. Maybe I am. But I figured a female detective had to have experienced her share of judgements.

But then, that was me making a judgement, too, wasn't it? And mine was based on the detectives in decades-old black and white movies. Even with the steps taken toward gender equality, the world hadn't come all that far. People still assumed women were weak. Soft.

Unable to protect themselves.

Okay, so Piper liked to tell me my best self-defense was thinking out loud. She said I'd run off any attacker if they could hear what was going on inside my head.

Rude, I know.

Also, maybe a little bit true.

"I know a bit about you," Detective Watson said, pulling me from my thoughts. "I've read the statement you made after finding the body. And I've looked at your record. You've been arrested a lot, but not for anything big."

"Can you tell my lawyer that?"

She chuckled again.

Darn it, I was starting to like her.

"I'm sure your lawyer loves working with you. You give her a lot of business." She raised a hand as if to stop anything I might say. "Your arrests have all come from trying to make the world a better place, not from making it more chaotic. But Detective Price's notes also say you're a pacifist. And, to be honest, you don't instill confidence in your ability to protect yourself."

"We turn here." I veered toward the upper path. "There's always a better way to solve things than with violence."

"My point exactly. That's why Detective Price wanted me to keep an eye on you. Well, he told me he was going to ask Detective Locke, and I suggested you might accept me more easily."

I nodded. Detective Locke had seemed friendly, but I had a feeling Detective Watson would be easier to have around. "So it wasn't because he's afraid I'm going to cause problems?"

Her eyes twinkled. "Are you?"

I hadn't meant to cause trouble in the first place. And I still wasn't convinced I'd done anything wrong. It's not like I told everyone I was investigating. I'd said the exact opposite, because that was the truth. And was it my fault if Detective Thinks-I'm-A-Wimp missed a key fact when he talked to the ladies at the housing office? "Not on purpose."

"It's interesting. Detective Price usually has to be persuaded to use department resources like this, and he usually delegates it to a uniform."

I squirmed under her curious gaze. "You're not a uniform."

"No. I'm not. Which is why I was surprised when—" She cut off at the sound of a shout.

"Octavia, there you are. I've been looking all over for you." Piper raced over. Well, if she was anyone else, she'd have been racing. But my friend's effortless diva-level stage presence didn't let her race, even if that's the energy she gave off.

"I was just coming to see you."

As if she didn't even see Detective Watson standing next to me, Piper took my elbow and propelled me into a stand of trees.

"Did you find something new when you were exploring?" I asked.

She shook her head impatiently.

A short distance later, the trees opened into a small—it wasn't a clearing, exactly. A larger space between trees? A break in the undergrowth? Something. "Did you clear this out?"

"Of course not, darling. I might have gotten dirt under my nails." She looked at her nails in case they'd managed to get dirty without her knowing.

"I just happened to find it."

She went over to a fallen log and sat down.

I joined her, but didn't say anything about the dirt her pants might pick up. Then I looked at my shadow. "Have a seat."

"Oh." Piper fluttered her lashes. "Who are you?"

"This is—"

"Irene. I'm a friend of Octavia's." Detective Watson cut me off before I could give her away.

Which I totally wouldn't have done.

Piper's eyes cut to me. "Since when are you friends with cops?"

I opened my eyes as wide as they would go. "What do you mean?"

"Never do that with your face again," she answered.

Huh. I'd heard that wide eyes were more trustworthy. Guess that was wrong.

"What gave me away?" Detective Watson—Irene—asked.

Could I call the detective by her first name? She'd just introduced herself with it, but she was a detective. She was here professionally.

Piper patted the log next to her and waited for the detective to sit down. "You're a little over-dressed, to be honest, Irene."

I guess that answered whether we called her by her first name or her title.

"It's jeans," Irene said again, brushing a lock of her sleek bob out of her face to tuck it behind an ear.

She looked so forlorn that I decided to change the subject. "Piper, why are we in the woods?"

"Oh! I heard something."

Irene was on her feet, turning in a careful circle as she peered into the trees. She'd pulled a gun from somewhere.

My hands went up on instinct.

"Sorry, Irene. I didn't mean I heard something now." Completely ignoring the gun, Piper pulled Irene back to the log. "I heard something earlier. About one of the suspects."

I kept my eyes carefully on Piper, trying to silently remind her there was a detective sitting beside her. "Xavier already told me."

"Only as much as I trusted him with." Piper smirked. "You have to hear the rest."

"Piper—"

She spoke over me, taking away any chance of stopping Detective Price from finding out I was talking about the murder after he told me to stay quiet.

Although it wasn't really me talking, was it? I wanted to believe he couldn't get mad if Irene told him my friend wanted to talk about it, but I had a feeling it was still going to land on my shoulders.

And my shoulders weren't used to anything heavier than a viola.

"Xavier told you Tatiana met with the symphony board," Piper started.

"He did." *Please don't let this come back to bite me.* "That's why she wasn't at the amphitheater when I went to meet her."

She wiggled her fingers together like an evil villain. "That's where you're wrong. The meeting was right after rehearsal, and Tatiana was only there for ten minutes. The board told her the only chance of Ludwig leaving the symphony was if he chose to go somewhere else."

"How mad was she?"

"You mean, was she murderous?" Piper's lashes fluttered in excitement. "She might have been. The board member I talked to—"

Flirted with, I was sure.

"— said she had a fit and stormed out."

"I'm beginning to understand exactly why Detective Price wanted me to stick with you." Irene moved from the log to sit on the ground in front of us. She probably just wanted a better view, but it felt like I was in trouble.

"Detective Price sent you?" Piper asked, her voice way too innocent.

"Don't get hung up on it," I warned.

They shared a look I didn't understand, then Irene went on as if Piper hadn't jumped in. "I know we're verifying Tatiana's alibi—we're verifying all the alibis—but I'll make sure the team knows about this."

"You're leaving?" I wasn't sure if I was happy about that or not.

On the one hand, I didn't need a babysitter.

On the other hand, if she stuck around I might actually become friends with a cop. Detective. Law enforcement person. Thing.

"No, you're stuck with me for the rest of the day." She gave me a strange look. "I'll send him a text."

"Octavia doesn't believe in texting." The fact that Piper's voice was bland did nothing to hide her amusement. "Or phones in general."

"That's—" Irene's typing thumbs stilled as she processed the idea. "Okay, it's not the craziest thing I've heard."

Well, that's good. She must hear all sorts of crazy things in her line of work. "That reminds me, Piper. Will you call Cora for me? I want to talk to her."

My best friend and my new almost-friend exchanged a look.

"Don't ask," Piper suggested.

"I can't help it. Curiosity is why I'm good at what I do." Irene turned her attention to me. "How are you going to talk to her if Piper's the one calling?"

Thirteen

THE DRIVE DOWN THE CANYON was uneventful, unless you happened to include the argument over who would drive. I tended not to linger on those things—they ate way too much positivity.

Irene won, of course. Piper couldn't believe Irene was giving up the chance to ride in her sporty little convertible, but there wasn't room for all of us in the two-seater.

I hadn't even suggested taking Betty, even though we'd have easily fit in my van with the groovy paint job. You might be thinking it's because I was embarrassed by Betty. You wouldn't be the first to think I should be. You also wouldn't be the first to be wrong about it.

No, I didn't suggest it because I could tell Irene needed that control. Not in a control-freak way. In a doing-her-job kind of way.

So instead of offering to drive, I hopped into the back of her government-issued black vehicle that was almost as big as my little house, leaving Piper to claim shotgun since she didn't get to drive.

Irene pulled up some kind of navigation program on the screen. "What's your grandmother's address?"

We'd decided to meet at Grandmother's home because it was the only place Cora and I both knew how to find. As a bonus, it was halfway-ish between the city and Aerie Pines. "I have no idea."

The two front-seaters shared another look.

If they kept that up, Irene might take my place as Piper's best friend by the time the day was over.

"Don't worry, I can get us there," I assured them. "You'll turn left at the base of the canyon. Then go left at the third gas station on the right. Make sure it's the one on the right. Don't wait for the third on the left or you go into this suburban maze full of one-way streets and it's impossible to find your way out of there. Then you take the seventh street on the right, the second left, and the fourth right, and you're there."

"Is that all?" Piper asked.

Irene just looked at me like I'd sprouted an extra set of arms.

Which, let's face it, would be super cool. Then I could pull out my viola and jam with myself on the piano or bass. I'd totally dig it. Maybe there was another way to make something like that work.

"It's a good thing the woman we're meeting already knows how to get there," Irene finally said.

"You realize people have travelled by landmarks for, like, forever, right?" I asked.

The drive could have been awkward, but Irene

let me control the radio through orders to Piper. Since it wasn't really the radio, but something where you could choose what songs to hear, I chose songs that let us—namely, me—pretend we were— I was—at a music festival. No, not a classical music festival. I practically lived at one of those, remember? Think more along the lines of folk music. And Irish drinking songs. And a bunch of stuff from the sixties.

I made sure Irene got all the turns right, and we pulled into Grandmother's circular brick driveway. I hopped out of the car—Irene had turned off the perp lock, and I can't explain the freedom of getting out of the back of a cop's car, even if it wasn't a cruiser, without waiting for the door to be opened from the outside—and waited for the others.

When they finally joined me, I knocked on the door.

It wasn't long before the door swung in. Grandmother's face lit with a smile, and she patted her silver chignon as if she was afraid some of the hair had escaped and would make a bad impression. "Octavia. This is a surprise."

"Hi Grandmother." I motioned at Piper and Irene. "I brought some friends to visit. There's one more on her way."

"Hi Mrs. Fields," Piper said.

"Piper. I haven't seen you in some time." Grandmother stepped to the side, letting the door swing wide. Her usual slacks and sweater set looked too warm for summer, but she always claimed she ran cool. "Well, come in."

Movement caught my eye and I paused to look at the old cherry tree. Up on the branch I'd used to climb out of the bedroom I stayed in when I visited as a teenager sat a fat squirrel. I reached out my hand and it darted away, not nearly so friendly as Frenzy.

I turned back to follow Piper and Irene inside.

"How's the property?" Grandmother asked as I stopped to kiss her cheek. "Is everything as it should be? There aren't any fallen trees that need to be removed, are there? Is it time to add more gravel to the drive?"

"The parts of it I've checked look fine. There are a couple of small trees that didn't make it through the winter, but we don't need to clean up nature, Grandmother. The fallen logs will give animals homes, and eventually break down to feed the earth. And the gravel levels looked fine to me."

Grandmother just shook her head at me. "I'll have someone come up and check it."

"I'd be happy to check it for you," Irene offered. She held out her hand. "I'm Detective Watson."

Grandmother shot me an amused look and straightened her already straight shoulders. "What's she done now?"

Irene glanced at me.

"Go ahead," I encouraged. "She'll find out eventually."

"Octavia found the body of a murder victim."

Grandmother's carefully made-up face paled. "Come in and sit down, then you can explain why that brought you to my door. You don't think she's a suspect, do you? I know she's been arrested before, but only for self-expression, which I've always encouraged."

The doorbell rang as Grandmother led Piper and Irene into the large front room while getting assurances that no, I wasn't a suspect, but just as a precaution they weren't taking any chances with my safety. I lagged behind to open the door for Cora.

I greeted her with a hug. "Thank you for meeting me."

"It got me out of the house." She hugged me back. "I can't stay long, the kids are with my mother."

We joined the others in the front room just as Grandmother disappeared through a different door.

"Piper, I haven't seen you in too long." Cora hurried across the room.

After Piper greeted her, she introduced Irene, leaving off the fact Irene was a detective. I wasn't sure if that was on purpose or not, but Irene didn't correct her. "Octavia was nice enough to let us tag along."

Grandmother came back in and set a tray on the low table between the couches. "I made the bundt cake this morning, and there's lemonade to go with it."

I should have known she was getting food. Grandmother was raised in a world where there were very specific expectations of women. They were expected to look a certain way, and act a certain way, and be overwhelmingly polite. She was always the perfect hostess, and usually had a freshly baked something or other sitting on the counter just in case anyone dropped by.

Once, the only time I remember her getting drunk—which she only did because she didn't realize I'd spiked her lemonade—she admitted it wasn't the kind of life she'd ever wanted. It was the reason she went toe-to-toe with my parents to keep them from trying to force me into a mold, not that they'd have been successful.

In her relaxed state, she told me she'd wanted to live. To do things like go to music festivals and travel the country in a van.

Which explained why she'd aided and abetted my right to live the kind of life she wished she'd dared to live.

It was also why she bought the land I lived on during the summers. She mostly left the twenty acres to my care, but occasionally she came up to visit. She pretended to be worried about me, but really she was looking for an excuse to sit in a camp chair in front of the fire pit and soak in the peace of the mountains.

Grandmother started a conversation with Piper while I turned to Cora. "How are you doing, really? And the kids?"

Cora massaged the lines skimming her forehead. Dark circles under her eyes told me she wasn't getting enough sleep. "It's been hard. Ludwig's mother keeps calling, insisting she should have the kids with her to help them through it. Something about assuming his visitations. I told her no. They just lost their father, they don't need to be pulled away from their mother as well."

I'd only met Ludwig's mother once, but it had been clear that her ego on her son's behalf was even bigger than the one he had for himself. "I don't think she can do that. His visits shouldn't be transferrable."

"I'm afraid I'm going to have to hire an attorney to stop her." Cora ran her hands down her thighs.

I glanced at Irene, who was thumb-typing into her phone. Hopefully she was telling Detective Price to take care of it.

"We'll make sure you have people on your side," I assured her. "Is there going to be a funeral, or are you doing a private memorial service? If it's a funeral, I'm sure some of the symphony members will want to be there."

Piper pulled a face behind Cora's back, but let the lie stand.

Cora reached for a glass of lemonade and downed the whole thing. As she set the glass back on the table, she sighed. "I suppose it's up to me to figure that out, isn't it? When he left me, I never thought I'd have to do this. But the police haven't released his body yet. I'm not sure what they're waiting for."

Irene cleared her throat. "I'm sure the medical examiner's team is just making sure they have everything they need."

"What about what I need?" Cora choked out. "I just need this to be over. Do you have any idea what I'm going through? People are coming out of the woodwork to ask for details about my ex-husband. Reporters waiting outside the apartment to yell questions as I try to get past. They keep asking why we were divorced, if he had enemies, if I thought it was an accident. I don't know what to say, so I try to push past them."

They wanted to know if she thought it was an accident? Did that mean Detective Price hadn't told her it was murder? Was he waiting for more proof, or had he just been so busy he hadn't made it over to see her?

He could've at least sent someone if he couldn't go himself.

"I'm sorry." Cora brushed at the tears leaving tracks in her makeup. Suddenly the dark circles under her eyes were more visible. "I'm so sorry. You were so nice to want to see me, to ask about *me*. To—to be friends with me, even though the divorce means I'm not part of the music world anymore."

I handed her a cloth napkin to use as a handkerchief and put a reassuring arm around her. "Detective Price and his team are working hard to figure out what happened. I'm sure they'll have it all worked out soon."

Cora dropped the napkin into her lap and reached for my hand. "Are you helping them?"

How was I supposed to answer that, especially with Detective Watson sitting there waiting to hear what I'd say? "Not officially."

She hiccuped. "But you're helping. You must be. Ludwig always said you were the best part of that symphony."

Piper's eyes widened and she looked ready to clock Cora.

I spoke before Piper could go all *I was his stand partner* on us. "I'm not part of the symphony anymore."

"But people talk to you," Cora insisted. "They always have."

I didn't agree, but I didn't disagree.

It was more like people usually forgot I was there, or thought I wasn't paying attention, and talked around me.

Cora nodded, as if that confirmed everything she was thinking. Taking a deep breath, she turned to Piper. "How was the safari?"

That was all the encouragement my friend needed to go into the details of her six-week-long trip.

Eventually, Cora looked at her watch. "It's been so nice to visit with all of you, but I really do need to go. I don't want to be away from the kids for too long."

Piper stretched her arms. "I should be getting back to Aerie Pines anyway. I need to get ready for tonight's concert."

Then we were all on our feet, and Grandmother was packing up slices of cake to send home with each of us.

As we pulled away, I couldn't help asking Irene why they hadn't let Cora know Ludwig had been murdered.

"We can't release information like that until we're sure." She paused as she turned onto the main road. "What makes you so sure it was murder, anyway?"

"Detective Price told me."

The part of her face I could see in the rearview mirror looked like she had a lot of things to say about that. Unfortunately, none of them made it past her lips.

Fourteen

BACK AT AERIE PINES, PIPER hurried off to eat something before warming up her fingers and changing into her summer concert white. The concert wouldn't start until dusk, but she had to be to the amphitheater an hour before that for a symphony meeting.

Irene hung back with me when Piper ran off, moving at a lazier speed and asking me to point out what each building was used for.

The large hotel where Ludwig had apparently been staying while he tried to get access to one of the cabins overlooked the parking lot. In a moment of weakness, Irene admitted they'd been to see his room but hadn't found anything of interest.

As we followed the path up toward the amphitheater we neared the ticket office on the left, but veered off in the other direction around the back of the gift shop.

Tucked up against the stream and forest on the other side of the green, the restaurant already looked busy. Even though it was a late concert, people liked to arrive early—to eat, or, if they had lawn tickets, to choose their spot before it got crowded.

We passed the group of administration buildings, then went up the hill to the next tier.

"I haven't been down there. Where does it go?" Irene asked, pointing to a smaller path that went up higher.

"That's the Lodge. A place musicians and staff can stay in just a room instead of an apartment or condo."

"Octavia," someone called.

I focused on the path in front of me. A woman with short-cropped hair raised a hand in greeting as she broke into a jog.

"I didn't expect to see you already," I said as she joined us. I introduced her to Irene. "Bethanne teaches at one of the summer music programs down the road."

Bethanne looked a little guilty. "I left my rosin in the back window of the car. It melted, of course, so I needed to buy more."

I winced. It wasn't the first time she'd done that. "Did it get all over your car?"

She shook her head. "I was lucky this time. Hey, I heard you found Ludwig. Are you okay?"

I nodded. Bethanne had met Ludwig, of course. Everyone around here seemed to know everyone else, but Bethanne hadn't known him well enough to truly care that he was dead.

Although, if we're being honest—and since you're kind of living in my head, I suppose there's no point in being anything but honest—even the people he knew best didn't seem to care he was gone. Except for Cora, of course, and that was more for the sake of their kids than because she still loved him.

Even though I sometimes thought she did. Still love him, I mean. I got the feeling she assumed they'd get back together after he went through his midlife crisis of only caring about himself.

Obviously that couldn't happen now.

Irene nudged me.

Oh, right. "I'm dealing with it."

"Did he have a heart attack?" Bethanne asked. She was more subtle about it than some people I could name—like Xavier and Piper—but she obviously just wanted the gossip. "I heard the man had a temper. That could have caused it, right?"

Irene shifted a tiny bit. "The authorities are still looking into it."

"Oh. Well. There's a rumor going around that it wasn't a health thing. Have you heard it? Some people think he was killed."

"I've heard that one." Maybe I should have told her I wasn't handling the whole thing very well so she'd have decided not to ask about it all. "I'm sure the detectives are looking into every possibility."

Bethanne shivered. "And you're helping them. I don't know how you can stand to get that close to it."

Who told her I was helping? I mean, I knew the symphony members were sure that's what was happening, but I didn't think Bethanne was very close to any of them. Had Xavier been saying things he shouldn't while I was gone? "I'm not actually helping. I just had to give a statement about finding him."

Her face fell. "Oh. Well, I don't know who to talk to then."

"About what?" Irene asked.

"One of the staff where I work is friends with Tammy Spencer in the housing office here. Do you know her?" Realizing she had an interested audience, Bethanne didn't wait for an answer. "Tammy told Lorraine that she doesn't know what to do, or who she can talk to without causing problems."

I purposely didn't look at Irene. "I don't think people are supposed to talk about an ongoing investigation."

Bethanne wobbled her head from one side to the other like a metronome. "Yes, well, she needs to tell someone, because it might be important."

I almost told her that Irene was one of the detectives, but somehow Irene could tell what I was going to do and shook her head. Not so much Bethanne would notice with her own head metronoming.

Bethanne leaned closer and spoke *sotto voce,* even though the nearest person couldn't possibly be listening to our conversation. "Tammy said her boss, the woman in charge of the housing office, was angry with that poor dead man."

Poor? That's the first time I'd heard that word applied to Ludwig.

"This woman was downgrading him to a single room instead of an apartment. She went off to find him and came back acting differently than normal—and just a few minutes later, you found the man's body." She lowered her voice even more. "Tammy's afraid her boss killed him."

"I talked to Vanessa and she didn't say anything about looking for him," I mused. She also hadn't mentioned that she was moving Ludwig to the Lodge.

If she found him and told him about that, he would have been furious. It would have meant he couldn't have the kids stay with him—as unpractical as the whole idea was in the first place—for more than a night or two without his neighbors getting annoyed at the extra noise the kids would certainly make.

Would he have lashed out at her? Could she have reacted by grabbing that bust and swinging it at him, either in self-defense or just to get him to leave her alone?

"I knew you were investigating, even though you said you weren't," Bethanne breathed.

"What? Oh, no," I hurried to add. "No, no, no. I just had a conversation with her. No investigating."

"Well, I guess I've left the information in good hands. Thank you, Octavia, now I won't have to worry about it. And if Tammy asks, I'll tell her you're taking care of everything." She swooped in and gave me a quick hug, then she hurried down the path.

"I—I didn't—I'm not—" My words were too late. She was getting smaller with every step.

"How did that happen?" Irene asked.

I turned on her. "What?"

"That woman searched you out to tell you about what Tammy Spencer's friend told her. Which is hearsay, by the way, until we confirm it." Irene's forehead crinkled in concentration. "You told her you weren't investigating. I heard you myself. But she still told you everything she knew."

Right? It would have made so much more sense for Tammy to reach out to Detective Trying-His-Darnedest-But-Getting-Thwarted-At-Every-Turn and tell him. She had his card. It would have been easy.

"What is it about you that makes people tell you things?" Irene continued.

I thought and thought. Finally, I shrugged. "Maybe people know I won't judge them, or they're drawn to my aura, or they just want to feel heard."

Irene shook her head. "I have to tell Detective Price about this."

"That people talk to me on their own and I'm not the one instigating it all? I hope he believes you more than he believed me when I told him that."

"What?" She laughed as she pulled out her phone. "Actually, I meant I needed to tell him what the woman said. But I'd be happy to tell him it wasn't your fault."

I inched away from the death machine. "I'll just stand over here while you call him."

"Don't be silly. You can stay right here and I'll send him a text." She focused on the screen as she typed. Then there was a quick back and forth as they discussed things without speaking.

Seriously, even if you can get past the other negative energy things about these little phones, how are you supposed to understand what people mean by what they say in a text when you can't see their expression? How do you know if they're teasing, or if they've had an epiphany, or if they're actually offended behind the polite words they type?

"Octavia?" Irene's voice did that funny thing that tells me people have asked a question I haven't answered.

"Hmm?"

"I need to speak with this woman. Vanessa."

I nodded.

"Will the housing office still be open?"

"I don't know, but we can check. It's just back in the administration buildings." I started back in the direction we'd come from. Then I paused. "Are you going to tell me I have to go stay in the shop while you talk to her?"

Irene held her phone out to me.

I leaned away from it, pulling my hands close to my chest. "What are you doing?"

"You don't have to touch it, just read what's on the screen."

Staying as far away from it as I could while still making out the words, I read the text from Detective Price.

> Do not let Octavia out of your sight. Her safety is your priority. Take her with you to talk to the housing woman. If you don't, Octavia will somehow manage to find out what happens anyway.

"Aw, he's sweet," I said as I backed a relatively safe distance away from the phone.

"Sweet. That's a new one. I bet even Jack's mother's never called him sweet," Irene muttered.

Jack? Oh, Detective Price. Huh. I hadn't even thought about what his first name might be. Was it on the card he'd given us? Probably.

Jack. Jack in the box. Jack be nimble. Jack of all trades.

I wasn't at all sure the name fit the detective.

Irene's phone buzzed again. She looked at the screen and laughed, then held it out to me.

I squinted until the words swam into focus.

> Try to keep her quiet, and don't let her hijack the interview.

Rude. I grabbed the pointy part of my glasses and straightened them. "I won't try to take over, but I can't promise not to say anything if Vanessa talks to me first."

Irene gave me a look, but didn't say anything.

I'm sure you realize what I was thinking.

No? Huh, maybe you haven't gotten to know me as well as I thought.

I was thinking Vanessa might be more comfortable talking to me than to Irene. First, because Irene was going to have to finally admit to someone that she was a detective in order to interview her. Second—and much more important, I'm sure you'll agree—Vanessa had already told me a lot more than she'd told the first detective who'd spoken to her. It made sense that she'd continue the trend.

Fifteen

THE HOUSING OFFICE DOOR WAS open, but from a quick peek inside, it was clear it wouldn't stay that way long. Tammy had her purse slung over her shoulder, and Vanessa was picking up a set of keys from her desk.

Irene knocked on the doorframe as she stepped inside. "Ms. Chambers?"

Vanessa's head came up, every line of her body marked by weariness. "We're closing. Whatever your problem is, it'll have to wait for tomorrow."

"I'm afraid not," Irene said. Her posture had changed, and you'd have to be blind to see her as anything other than the detective she was.

Tammy's gaze slid past Irene to land on me. She startled as recognition crossed her face. She froze for a beat, then moved faster as she crossed the room and squeezed between Irene and me. "Have a good night, Vanessa."

Irene stepped farther into the room. I followed her, closing the door for good measure.

At the sound of the latch, Vanessa glanced at me. Her grip on the keys tightened until her knuckles turned white. "I already told you more than I should have. I have nothing to add."

I bit my lip to hold back a flood of words.

"Have a seat." Irene's words were a demand instead of an invitation.

Vanessa's shoulders went back. "We're closing. You can come back tomorrow, but I'll just tell you the same thing I'll say right now: If you want gossip, you came to the wrong place. I don't have time for that kind of thing."

"The longer you fight the conversation, the longer it'll take." Irene pointed to the chair, then she introduced herself, including her title. "Sitting down and getting it over with is your fastest way out that door."

As Vanessa lowered herself into the chair she shot me a dark look. "I should have known you were one of the people who can't keep their mouths shut. This place is crawling with them."

Me? I wasn't a gossip.

I know you probably think I am. I mean, I spend my days with Piper and Xavier, who are arguably the biggest gossips in this place that's apparently *crawling* with gossips.

But, generally, I keep my—well, fine, I don't keep my thoughts to myself. It's hard, that's why. They just kind of spill out of me. But I try.

Talking about other people, though, is something I usually leave to other people. Sure, I talk with my friends and employees, and we maybe say things we shouldn't, but it's just between us.

Okay, so maybe I do gossip. A little. It's not as if I'm hurting anyone. Just ask Piper. I carry spiders outside when they bother people, but I'm just as happy to let them weave their delicate webs high up in the corner as I am to banish them. If I can live and let live with spiders and all their legs, of course I can do the same with human beings.

"Octavia is the least of your problems." Irene leaned against the desk.

Vanessa looked up at the detective and clenched her jaw.

Uh-oh. This wasn't going to work. People like Vanessa, who took offense at a simple statement, weren't likely to give cops or detectives—or anyone in charge—what they were after without a fight.

I'd seen people arrested at a simple, peaceful protest turn into vicious animals when they were cornered for a statement at the police station.

Trust me, that's not the way to get released quickly. Or to be treated as a visitor instead of a prisoner, for that matter.

I tried to catch Irene's eye. It didn't work. She was too busy trying to intimidate Vanessa.

Did I let her handle it, or would it be better to help soften things? I could be the harmony that grounded and eased the intensity of Irene's searing melody.

Vanessa was visibly closing herself to Irene.

If we were going to get anywhere other than a ride to a jail cell, someone had to do something. Since Irene didn't seem to see that, it was up to me. "Look, Vanessa, we know you're ready to go home. It's been a long day for all of us. But, see, here's the thing. People are talking. Not because everyone around here's a gossip, but because someone died."

Vanessa snorted in spite of herself. "That man brought it on himself, all high and mighty. In fact, you remind me of him just a bit."

Irene's eyes narrowed.

I hurried on before the detective could make things harder than they needed to be. "It doesn't matter how annoying Ludwig could be, his death is tragic. If things don't get straightened out, there's a chance the pall of his death could ruin Aerie Pines. Then we'd all be out of work."

"Maybe we should be," Vanessa muttered. "I wouldn't miss the complaining. It's just one problem after another with these musicians."

"Be fair. They're not all bad. You just get stuck with the complaints because this is the office people are supposed to bring them to. If it's that annoying for you, I'm sure you could find a job doing something you like more."

Several expressions crossed her face so quickly I couldn't make them out. Like music notes on the page seem to stop making sense for a second when you lose your place on a piece you're just learning and have to try to catch up.

"Listen, Vanessa, there's another rumor going

around, and instead of just believing it, we came to ask you to clarify something." I turned to Irene so she could be the one to ask the questions.

I didn't expect it to keep her from telling me I'd stepped on her toes, but maybe it would soften her enough that she wouldn't go complaining to Detective Price about it. Somehow I didn't think he'd be as understanding, especially after the way he told Irene I'd try to take over.

Ridiculous man. As if I could hijack anything.

"Where were you just before the body was found?" Irene asked.

Oh, sweet Brahms, what was she doing? Treating Vanessa like a suspect, even if she was one, was only going to make things worse.

"The thing is," I said, trying to keep the interview from going downhill, "someone said you were looking for Ludwig."

Irene turned on me.

I'd never seen that look on her face. And okay, sure, I hadn't known her long—at all—but that was the kind of look reserved for either really good friends, or people who didn't care if they became your friend.

Had I just imagined we were getting along?

No, that couldn't be it.

"You already know the man was insisting he deserved a cabin," Vanessa said. She seemed to have missed the tension in the air.

Which was saying something, because was it ever thick.

"The hotel called and told me he couldn't keep staying there. The room was booked starting tomorrow, and they expected me to get him out of there."

"So what did you do?" Irene asked. At least this time she had the smarts to make it sound conversational instead of like she was interrogating the woman.

"I couldn't give him a cabin. Even if he was important enough to have a whole entourage with him, they'd already been assigned. We've got someone from Hollywood staying this week because of tonight's concert, and we have composers and VIPs coming in all summer." Vanessa reached over and toyed with the pens sitting in a cup on the desk.

Irene reached over and moved the cup out of reach.

You know, I've always kind of thought my patience was good. Legendary, almost, or so Piper's said a bunch of times. But Irene was pushing past where it ended. Somehow, that woman was able to cut through it as if it didn't exist.

That was pure, raw talent, and one I didn't appreciate. If toying with pens made Vanessa comfortable enough to tell us what we came to find out, it wouldn't hurt to let her do it.

With the pens out of reach, Vanessa dropped her hands into her lap. "He wasn't happy with the apartment, and—well, it was petty of me, I realize that, but—I assigned him to a room at the Lodge. The smallest room I could find."

I tried not to laugh, really I did, but I could totally picture how he'd take that slap in the face. "And you went to tell him about it."

Vanessa nodded. "I did. I looked all over the place. I was at the amphitheater, and the auditorium, and the concert hall. I even went to the hotel."

"What did he say when you told him you'd downgraded his lodging?" Irene asked.

"You don't think I killed him, do you?" Vanessa shook her head. "I admit I was looking forward to seeing how angry he'd be when he found out he wasn't getting his way. That man thought he was the most important person on this mountain. But I couldn't have done anything to him. I never found him."

I wasn't sure if Irene believed her.

I wasn't sure if *I* believed her, either.

Because if Ludwig had stood there while anyone, let alone someone he'd see as so far beneath him, told him he didn't get something he thought he deserved, well, I think we all knew it wouldn't go well.

Of course he would lash out. That's what he did. I'd never seen him lash out with more than words, or the way he poured his anger into the music, but that didn't mean he hadn't snapped. And he'd made such a big deal about how he thought he deserved more that I could picture him getting really upset.

The question was, if he'd gotten upset and aimed that anger at Vanessa, could she have decided to put a stop to it?

Sixteen

Let's just pretend Irene—Detective Watson—didn't go and tattle to Detective I-Told-You-She-Was-Trouble, okay?

All you really need to know is that no one listened when I tried to explain that Vanessa wasn't going to give up anything if she was too busy reacting to glowers and being put under more stress than a first year violin student asked to perform the Mendelssohn Violin Concerto.

No, they were too busy trying to impress upon me the importance of their way of doing things.

Can you hear that? It's the sound of my eyes rolling.

Piper was on my side when she walked in on our argument, thank goodness. Someone had to have my back.

Okay, argument really isn't the right word for it. The detectives thought they were giving me a dressing down—Detective Watson in person, Detective Price through a video call thing on

Irene's phone. I stood well away from that, but she kept following me around holding the phone toward me so I couldn't get away from his voice.

"Are you sure you want to stay, with everything going on?" I asked Irene as I spread a blanket on the grass. "I'll understand if you need to rush off and interrogate another suspect, or play with the murder board I'm sure Detective Price has set up. Or if you just want to go home. I know it's getting late."

It wasn't actually late yet, but I had to offer her the out in case she wanted one.

The sun was almost down, and the audience gathering for the night's concert was getting bigger by the minute. Luckily Hector's team had been nice enough to make sure no one claimed my normal spot back toward the restaurant, behind the speakers set to project the music across the grass.

She reached down to fix a corner of the blanket that had folded over on itself. "Nice try, but you're not getting rid of me that easily. I told Detective Price that I'd make sure you got home safely."

As if I didn't get myself home safely every single day. Or at least on the days I chose to go home.

"He's my boss. I had to tell him about what happened at the housing office," she said.

"You can tell people anything you want."

"Even if he wouldn't see it in my notes in the app we use, Jack is smart. He'd figure it out pretty quick." Irene sat on the blanket and pulled snacks out of the bag she'd brought along after we went

back to her giant black SUV for an extra blanket—
she was afraid she'd get cold sitting still this high in
the mountains after dark. She held out a chocolate
bar as if it was a peace offering.

I recognized the wrapper and reached for it.

"Does that mean I can still be your friend?" she
asked.

"You keep the good kind of chocolate on hand.
I guess that means you're okay." The chocolate was
fair trade. A cacao farmer-owned company that
made the best chocolate I'd ever tasted and built
schools for the small communities where the
farmers lived. How could I stay mad at her?

She smiled. "Are you sure you want to sit here?
I'm not sure we'll be able to see the stage."

She was joking. I could see at least half of it.
Sure, the rest of it was blocked by the pillars
holding up the roof that covered the fancy-pants
seats, but I didn't need to see the viola section
anyway. If I saw the principal violist's cues I might
forget I didn't have my own instrument and try to
come in on my part. It was bad enough my fingers
tried to play my part even if there weren't strings
under them. I didn't need my brain adding to the
mess.

"If I lean this way I can see a little bit more,"
Irene said.

"These are the best seats in the house," I
promised.

The look she gave me said she wasn't convinced,
but she was choosing to trust me.

"Tonight's concert is special. That's why it's starting so late. It needs to be dark. From here we'll get to see the full effect of the show."

Irene pulled out a bag of licorice. Well, it was red, so it wasn't truly licorice, but I've been told most people don't make that distinction. She eased a rope out of the package and waved it in the air to emphasize her words. "What music are they playing? Just so you know, my musical career ended when I accidentally broke two of my piano teacher's fingers, so I'm not super familiar with much beyond *Hot Cross Buns*."

I tried not to wince at the idea of broken fingers. We were being friendly, and I didn't want to make Irene feel bad, even if I felt bad for her teacher. "They're doing themes from famous space movies."

Musicians had started wandering onto the stage to warm up. I watched as Piper sat in the concert-master chair.

Hopefully no one was giving her a hard time about that. She deserved the chair. She'd worked hard, and was a fantastic leader. I just wish she didn't get to sit there because of Ludwig's death.

"So they're performing when it's dark so we can see into space?" Irene asked.

I shook my head. "No, but they should totally do that. They could bring in a bunch of big telescopes and let people gaze into space as the music plays. That would blow people's minds."

I bet they could fit a lot of telescopes out here,

and there wasn't a lot of light pollution on the mountain, which meant they'd have a primo viewing experience.

Could the symphony afford to bring in something like that? I bet if they just put out the invitation for astronomers—professional ones and hobbyists—they'd have a lot of people volunteer to share the use of their telescopes. People loved introducing things they were passionate about to a new audience.

And it might bring in new fans for the symphony.

I should really share the idea with someone for next year. Or maybe I should get Piper to share it. People didn't give her the same *do-you-know-you're-crazy?* looks as they tended to give me.

"So what makes tonight's concert special?" Irene asked.

"What?" I focused on her as she motioned to the stage. "Oh, right. They're going to turn out all the lights except the ones clamped on to the music stands, and do a laser light show to the music. From here we can see all the projectors."

She looked around to see if she could make out the projectors. "A laser show? I thought symphony concerts were more stuffy than that. No offense."

As if I'd take offense to that. I'd sat through—and played—my share of *stuffy* concerts, but those didn't happen too much anymore. "Some concerts are serious. Like, really deep. But there are different concert series. Some are more fun and meant to entertain anyone, not just music aficionados.

Besides, this is the summer season. It's easier to do things like this when you're outdoors."

Applause rippled through the audience as the conductor walked on stage.

The next two hours did a lot to change Irene's opinion of symphony music. The light show was spectacular, and the bigwig who'd scored the cabin Ludwig had wanted was a big star in one of the famous movies the symphony had featured. I had no idea who the guy was, since I wasn't big on movies, but Irene was suitably impressed.

Maybe, if we stayed friends once the detectives figured out who killed Ludwig, I'd invite Irene to the movie concert.

No, it's not what you're thinking. Well, if you're thinking they play music from movies it isn't. What they do is play the soundtrack while a movie plays. I'd have to look and see what movie they were featuring this year.

Of course I knew we might not really be friends. I said *if*. But *if* we were actually friends, not just friendly because it was convenient, it could be fun.

There was always room for more friends.

Maybe the whole detective team would want to come to the movie night. Detective Locke looked like the kind of guy who might enjoy movies.

And Detective Price, well, he didn't look like he was easily amused, so he might not enjoy it. On the other hand, when he'd smiled that Detective Devastating smile, he looked like the kind of guy who'd linger over every possible enjoyment just to prolong the moment.

I reminded myself I wasn't supposed to be thinking of the detective in any way other than as the person solving the murder of a fellow musician.

That warm spot in my belly had the nerve to call me a liar.

Maybe I'd had too much of Irene's delicious fair trade chocolate.

The grassy area around the amphitheater was noisy as people gathered up their blankets and chairs and tried to beat each other to the parking lot to see who could get on the road the fastest.

Piper found us just as Irene was helping me fold the blanket we'd been sitting on. "Ladies, what we need is a girls night."

I glanced at Irene. "I'm sure the detective here wants to be getting home so she's awake for work in the morning."

No, I wasn't trying to leave her out. What would make you think that? I was trying to be thoughtful.

"We can do it at Octavia's place," Piper continued as if I hadn't spoken. She tucked her arm through Irene's. "Come on, it'll be fun."

Irene grinned. "Actually, Jack gave me tomorrow off."

"Jack?" Piper asked.

"Detective Price," I corrected. What was wrong with them? He was the lead detective. He was in charge. You don't insult the person in charge by leaving off their title. You left off their actual name before you ditched the title.

Piper's head spun toward me. "You know his first name?"

"Irene mentioned it earlier," I mumbled. He still didn't feel like a Jack in my head, even if I were to leave off the title. Which I wouldn't. Because he hadn't told me to.

Which was strange, when I stopped to think about it. Names were just a label. I chose to use people's first names all the time. It took away barriers that shouldn't be there in the first place. Made us equals.

So why did it seem so important to keep that "detective" at the front of Jack Price's name?

Sure, I knew these law enforcement types liked to remind people they were in charge when normal people like me bent the rules. But that hadn't stopped me from getting on a first name basis with Irene.

That spot in my belly was warm again. I wasn't going to think about what that meant.

Irene thoughtfully intervened. "He can be hard to deal with, but he's very good at his job. If you're both up for something tonight, I'd enjoy it. I promised him I'd see Octavia home safely, anyway."

"I guess we're going to my place." Was my laundry still hanging on the line? That tended to make people uncomfortable for some reason. "I just need to go up to the shop and get my bike."

"I'll come pick you up in the morning," Piper said. "We should just go."

It didn't make the most sense, and we wouldn't be getting out of the parking lot anytime soon, but I knew when a fight wasn't worth fighting. "Groovy."

As expected, getting onto the road was a mess, but most of the cars were turning the other direction instead of climbing higher up the mountain toward the pass. That meant once we were out of the parking lot, things went a lot faster.

I pointed out the narrow driveway that almost disappeared in the darkness, and Irene turned and made her way slowly off the road. The gravel crunched under the tires, and as we neared the clearing something moved in the glow from the headlights.

I leaned forward. "Stop!"

Irene slammed on the breaks. "What?"

But I was already out of the SUV and hurrying forward.

Frenzy stood on his hind legs in the middle of the road. As I neared, he started chittering at me, his little hands waving frantically.

No, not over his head like he was trying to get my attention or anything like that. He's a squirrel, not a diva. It was more like short, abrupt motions in front of his chest.

"What's wrong?" Irene asked. She and Piper had gotten out of the SUV to see what I was doing.

I shook my head. "I don't know. I've never seen him act like this."

"You . . . know this squirrel?" she asked.

"It's her pet. Kind of." Piper's smile made it all the way into her voice. "You know Octavia."

I chose not to point out that Frenzy had befriended me, not the other way around. Mainly because Frenzy had dropped to all fours and was running toward me. He ran up me as if I was his favorite tree and lay spreadeagle on top of my head.

"Does he usually sit on your head?" Piper asked.

"Of course not. Something has him worked up." I reached up to try to reassure my little friend. "Maybe he's worried about the extra car being here. We should walk the rest of the way."

Irene grumbled, but it seemed to be more for show than anything.

I mean, it wasn't like we had far to go.

The closer we got to the clearing, the tighter Frenzy held on. When the trees opened up, it was clear why.

Something had been here while I'd been gone.

Seventeen

My laundry was no longer on the line, and it wasn't because I'd put it away. Nope, it had been strewn around the clearing. Normally, I'd think it might have been the wind. Except it hadn't been windy, and the clothes had been spread in every direction.

And it wasn't just the laundry.

The pile of firewood had been rearranged. It wasn't tidy anymore. It wasn't even a pile. It had been scattered the same as the laundry. The little camp stove I'd set up for when I wanted to cook outside instead of in my tiny house had been overturned. The quilt from my bed was in a pile in the house's open doorway—and I was sure I'd closed the door.

I took a step forward, but suddenly Irene was blocking my way and pointing back the way we'd come.

"From the look on your face, this isn't how you expected to find things. Has this happened before?" Irene had made the full transformation into Detective Mode.

I shook my head, carefully so I wouldn't dislodge Frenzy. Then I reached up and pulled him off my head and tucked him in to cuddle against my chest.

"Thank goodness you weren't hurt. I bet you had the sense to stay out of the way while this happened. And then you came to warn us!"

"Do you think they're still here?" Piper asked. She sounded almost as excited at that prospect as she'd been by the idea that she was a suspect in Ludwig's murder.

"Focus, ladies." Irene didn't sound amused by the situation.

I guess if you were always dealing with the worst of humanity, you'd jump to all the worst conclusions when you found a mess like this. "Occasionally something will blow off the clothesline, but I've never come home to this kind of mess."

"Get back in the car and stay there until I come get you." Irene had pulled a gun from somewhere.

I'd obviously missed a magic trick, because there hadn't been anywhere obvious for her to be packing that thing, and after the gun had seemed to materialize earlier when we were in the woods, I'd been looking.

Piper pulled on my arm.

Irene looked like she wanted to say something more as my friend pulled me away from the clearing, but her phone was already halfway to her ear. "Jack, we have a problem."

"She called *Jack,*" Piper whispered as she dragged me to the SUV. "I hope he's going to come save us."

"You're married," I reminded her. "And there's no reason for him to save us. Irene is here, and whoever did this is probably long gone. It was probably just a lost hiker, anyway."

Piper opened the passenger door and hopped in, taking shotgun again without calling it first. "Do you really think a lost hiker would mess things up like that?"

"I've heard stranger things." I climbed into the back, keeping Frenzy close. I cooed at him. "You're going to get extra nuts for coming to tell us about it. Yes, you are."

His job done, Frenzy settled on my lap and fell asleep.

Piper and I sat in the dark vehicle, neither of us ready to break the quiet.

It was possible that animals had moved things around. A herd of deer could be responsible. Maybe Buttercup had a party while I was gone all day. I hadn't even thought to look for hoof prints.

"I'm glad we came home with you," Piper finally said. She looked at me over her shoulder. "What would you have done if you'd come home to that on your own? You don't even have a phone to call for help."

I couldn't tell her I'd have just gone inside to bed and waited until morning to clean up. Not because it wasn't true, but I knew Piper well enough to know she'd never forgive me if she thought I was putting myself in danger.

Not that I thought there was any danger. Not really.

Sure, there was a murderer lurking around somewhere, but that couldn't have anything to do with this. Most people didn't even know where I lived in the summer. The winter, either, but since *I* never knew where I was going to be in the winter, that didn't count.

No, if this was related to Ludwig's death, they'd have gone after the shop. You know, *if* anyone thought I was worth attacking. Which I totally wasn't. Even if I'd gotten that strange note in the mail.

"Octavia?"

Oh. Right. "I could always have ridden my bike back to Aerie Pines and spent the night at the shop."

She made a funny noise in her throat.

"Or I could have stayed with you," I added.

"That's better."

We both sat taller as Irene came toward us. She didn't stop. Instead, she walked back toward the road.

"Do you think she'll find anything?" Piper asked.

"Of course not. There's nothing to find, Piper. There's nothing to worry about." I almost believed my words. It would have been easier, though, if Frenzy hadn't come to let us know something had happened.

But as long as I pretended that didn't mean something was wrong, we were fine.

Headlights pulled up behind us. Someone got out and slammed the door closed.

"He came to rescue us." Piper's excitement was back.

I leaned toward her and tapped the tip of my finger against her wedding ring. "Married."

"I am, but you aren't. You should definitely be flirting with him."

Detective Oh-So-Flirtable stalked through the darkness toward the SUV we were—let's not say hiding—sitting in.

I swallowed hard. "I don't need anyone to flirt with."

Piper started to say something, but the door beside her opened.

"Ms. Holland." He looked past her. His eyes swept over me as if looking for injuries. "Ms. Fields. Come with me."

With a nod, Piper climbed out. Frenzy jumped up and followed her out.

"Not happening." I crossed my arms over my chest. "Irene told us to stay here until she came to get us. You're not her, so. . ."

Detective Price opened the back door, rested his hands on the seat beside me, and leaned in.

I couldn't help it. I breathed him in, and it was like taking a hit. He smelled woodsy and clean, with a hint of sandalwood and spice.

My mouth watered.

"Octavia."

"Hmm?"

His pupils contracted. "Get. Out. Of. The. Car."

"Okay," I squeaked.

Squeaked? I'd never squeaked in my life. Not even that time I'd breathed in the helium from two balloons. My voice hadn't squeaked so much as it had just gone into a range where only dogs could hear it.

Detective Delectable backed up just enough for me to slide between the black t-shirt hugging his chest and the frame of the truck. Car. Thing.

We stood there for a breath before he stepped back, leaving me feeling alone and vulnerable.

My mind ran through every cuss I could remember, just to prove it could. I could not be attracted to the man.

Okay, clearly that wasn't true, because I was.

I couldn't allow myself to act on that attraction. Nope, nuh-uh, no way.

He was a cop. Cops didn't go for flings with girls like me.

And girls like me didn't throw themselves at cops.

No, what was happening here wasn't actual attraction. It was the adrenaline, that's what it was.

Adrenaline.

Coming home to find things a little ransacked would spike anyone's adrenaline, so that made sense.

Perfect sense.

I just hoped Piper hadn't noticed that adrenaline-induced *moment*. She'd gone to talk to Irene, so she'd have had to hear the quiet, haunting melody of attraction from afar.

"Detective Watson cleared the scene," Detective Price said as he started up the drive.

I latched onto the obvious lifeline. "There wouldn't be anyone there. It was obviously just a lost hiker having some fun, or maybe some animals."

From the corner of my eye I could see him shaking his head before I finished speaking. "Detective Watson doesn't think so. I'm inclined to go with her feelings on the matter. She has good instincts."

I have good instincts, too, and mine were telling me it wasn't the time to push my opinion.

"Walk me thorough it," he said.

"Through what?"

"Getting here. What you found. The whole thing."

As I filled him in on my version of the events, Piper and Irene joined us.

"Octavia would never leave things a mess like that," Piper chimed in. I almost missed the wink she sent me. "Tidiness is her single nod to normalcy."

Gah. Forget adrenaline. The whole moment back there was probably because of Piper's influence. Maybe she even orchestrated it.

Oh, Shostakovich. Piper was the one who wanted to come to my place tonight—she's the one who suggested we have a girls night. She'd hurried off earlier, presumably to get some dinner and spend time with her husband before the concert, but there'd been time, if she'd wanted, to come here.

It would have been easy for her to slip down the trail by the hotel and be back in the parking lot while Irene and I took our time.

Had she planned this? Would she do something like that?

I glanced at her. She was busy listening to some exchange between the detectives.

If she was trying to play matchmaker—which she'd totally do, by the way, she loved creating harmonies between people—she wouldn't have any qualms about messing things up.

She probably thought it was a perfect ruse. Conveniently invite a detective along when we stumble across the mess she'd made.

It made sense. I hadn't seen anything damaged, just moved around. Messed up.

And she'd lied to Detective Price. She always complained that I left things a mess, just because I didn't put something away if I thought I was going to need it again soon.

Now I was doubly glad she hadn't noticed that thing, whatever it was, between Detective Price and me.

As for Detective Price, he was walking as if he

expected to be attacked at any second, even though Irene had cleared the scene.

I hung back, letting the others walk ahead of me. It didn't take long for Piper to notice and drop back to join me.

The detectives glanced at us, but gave us a smidgen of privacy by letting us stay two steps behind them.

"Are you okay?" Piper asked.

I tried to tell her off with my eyes, but it must have been too dark for her to notice. I lowered my voice to a hiss. "What did you do?"

"What?"

I grabbed her arm and let the detectives get a few more steps away from us before whispering in her ear. "You haven't flirted with the man once, and you keep hinting I should."

"If you think I'm only hinting, we have a communication problem," she said.

I poked her in the side so she'd lower her voice. "Well, stop. I don't need a man in my life."

She shrugged. "Life's more fun if you have one."

I refused to smile. She didn't deserve a reaction. "Did you do this?"

"What?" Her eyes filled with what looked like genuine confusion, but I'd been wrong before.

"Did you come here and make a mess just so he'd have to come over and play rescuer?"

She laughed so loud the detectives stopped to watch. Luckily for her, when she spoke, her voice was so soft it would need more than a few *ps* to mark the volume if it was written on sheet music. "I wish I'd been that clever. But no, it wasn't me."

Well. That was a real downer. If Piper wasn't responsible for the mess, that meant the detectives were right and someone I didn't know had put their hands on my clean laundry.

Eighteen

DETECTIVE PRICE STOOD BESIDE MY fire pit, his feet planted wide, hands on his hips as he surveyed the mess. "And none of you noticed anything? Nothing unusual, no movements, something disappearing into the trees?"

"Just the squirrel," Piper said.

Detective Price did something strange with his mouth. It almost looked like a grimace, but who could grimace about something as cute as a squirrel?

"His name is Frenzy," I added. Then, before his face could do anything else weird, I hurried on. "There wasn't anything else, just the mess."

He nodded, as if glad for the chance to get back on track. "Any footprints?"

Irene took over. "There are depressions in the soil all over the place. Octavia's footprints are everywhere, but I didn't see any others."

"How did you know they were—?" His eyes drifted to my bare feet. "Oh. Right."

We all watched as he prowled around the area that amounted to my front yard. He stopped to look at a couple of the logs, going so far as to pull out tweezers and little plastic bags to take something from them as evidence.

"I have cloth bags, or beeswax wraps," I offered. "You know, keep the plastic to a minimum."

The look he gave me spoke volumes. All the kind of things that meant he thought I was crazy, and I should stay back and let him do his job, and whatever that moment between us before had been wouldn't repeat itself with someone who couldn't keep her nose out of things.

"I hope you at least recycle," I mumbled as I glared back at him.

"Should I bag the clothing?" Irene asked.

I stepped in front of her. "You're not taking my favorite shirt."

"Take a look at them, but I don't think you'll find anything," Detective Price said. He managed to meet my gaze, which means I probably need to work on my glare. "We shouldn't have to take anything important. Have you checked inside?"

"No, Irene sent us to hide as soon as we got here."

"You can go inside now, but I'd like to come with you." He held up a hand to stop the protest that was still forming on my lips. "I just want to be there in case you notice anything Detective Watson might have missed."

Ha! I'd seen how these detectives moved through the world. They didn't miss anything. On the other hand, it couldn't hurt to have Detective Muscles along in case something went wrong.

I made my way to the itty-bitty deck. "Can I pick things up?"

"As long as you let me take pictures before you move anything." Detective Price pulled out his phone and snapped some pictures of the quilt in the doorway, then motioned me forward. "If you notice anything out of place, like a footprint on that, let me know."

There didn't appear to be any marks on the fabric, but I wouldn't be sleeping with it until I'd had a chance to wash it. I glanced back at the clothes strewn across the clearing. Looked like I'd be doing laundry again in the morning anyway.

Inside, dishes were scattered on the little counter, and a couple of plates had been smashed on the floor. They weren't sentimental, but they'd been bright and cheerful. Maybe I could use the pieces to make a wind chime or some mosaics. I opened a narrow cupboard and pulled out a small broom and dustpan and set to work cleaning it up so I wouldn't cut my feet on the shards.

"Can I look around?" Detective Nosy asked.

"Knock yourself out."

As I tidied the kitchen area, Detective Price poked around my home, making comments as he went.

When he climbed up the ladder to look into the

sleeping loft, he said, "Other than the missing quilt, everything looks tidy."

He picked books off the floor and set them back on the shelves. "I didn't take you for a reader."

I smirked. "That just means you're normal. There's a lot you don't take me for that you probably should."

His eyes darkened, but before things could get weird he moved on to look in the bathroom. "There might be a problem here."

I put the broom away. "What did they do?"

"It appears someone has stolen your shower."

"Is that all?" I reached over and reorganized some of the books he'd picked up. "It's fine. I have an outdoor shower."

You know that feeling where you're convinced someone is watching you? It's like you can feel eyes burning into the back of your skull. Yes? Then you know how I felt right then.

I turned my head.

Yep, his eyes were on me, and he wasn't even blinking. "You shower outside?"

"Of course. If you look out the bathroom window, you can see the shower. Or just go outside and walk around the back."

Detective Disbelief disappeared into the -. When he came back, he didn't look any more impressed by the idea of an outdoor shower than he'd been when he'd gone in.

"You need to keep an eye out for any voyeurs. You're out there where anyone can see you, and you never know what will go through a person's mind if they stumble on a scene like that." His stern look was nothing I hadn't seen before.

Piper had tried to convince me the outdoor shower was a bad idea. My parents had tried. Men I'd dated had tried, although I always got the idea they thought the whole thing was titillating.

The only person who'd never blinked at the idea was my very proper grandmother. All she'd done was hire someone to come set things up so I could use solar panels to heat the water.

Detective Price stepped so close I had to look up to see his face. "I mean it, Octavia. There are bad people in the world."

"There are good people, too. You'll always find what you're looking for," I reminded him. Then, because I couldn't seem to stop myself, I leaned forward. "I'm in the middle of nowhere. To get to me from that side, someone would have to cross the stream over there and come through the Oregon grapes under those aspens, which I don't see anyone doing quietly."

He took a deep breath. "I don't know how you've survived like this for as long as you have."

I grinned and stepped back, away from his scent that made me want to crawl into his arms.

Nope. Not going to happen. It was just adrenaline from the night's excitement. That's all.

Keeping my grin in place, I added a chuckle. "Careful. You're starting to sound like my parents."

He wasn't. He sounded all concerned, where my parents had stopped trying concerned a long time ago. They went right for annoyed disbelief, paired with questions along the line of *what will people think of you?*

Which was ridiculous, because if my parents had bothered to get to know me, they'd know I didn't care what people thought.

Detective Price glanced at his phone. "I have all the pictures I need in here. I think it's time the four of us sat down for a conversation."

On the way out, I grabbed a box from under my chair.

Piper had lit a fire while we'd been checking inside the house, so we sat on logs around the flames. I opened the box and passed around the collapsible toasting forks, along with makings for s'mores.

Piper jumped on them and had a marshmallow roasting immediately, even though she knew she'd get a better toast on the marshmallow if she waited for coals.

Well, I hoped she knew that by now. I'd told her so many times we could set it to music and turn it into a canon.

Irene gamely loaded a marshmallow onto her fork, but Detective Price just held his toasting fork like he wanted to jab someone in the throat with it.

"I got pictures of everything before you got here," Irene told him as she held the marshmallow toward the flames. "I'll send you a file."

He ignored her. "I need to know what you've all been doing today."

"Well, you know about this morning," I reminded him. "After lunch, you sent Irene to follow me around."

"And now I'm asking for her report."

I pretended to lock my lips closed and tucked the imaginary key into his hand.

He didn't look happy about that. Instead of doing any of the endless things he could have done with that imaginary key, he tightened his fist and turned to Irene. "Well? You took Octavia to talk with the lady at the housing office. Is there anything she said that you didn't tell me about? Anything that would end with her being threatened again?"

"No. Jack, Octavia was standing right next to me when I told you all that. If you think, even for a second, that she wouldn't have jumped in and added something I forgot, even though she was angry with me for telling you about it, then you haven't really met her." She pulled her flaming marshmallow out of the fire and blew out the flames.

I tried not to shudder. Why would anyone turn a marshmallow into ash when they could get a nice golden toast on the outside with only a little more effort?

Piper cleared her throat. "Look, I wasn't with them when they met with Vanessa, but I spent most of the afternoon with them. Octavia didn't do anything she shouldn't have."

"Obviously, she did." Detective Price looked around pointedly.

"Look, Jack, she could have upset anyone." Piper ignored the way Detective Price froze at her use of his name. "Maybe someone wanted a better deal on something at the shop, or thought she should be able to get a repair done sooner. There's any number of reasons someone could be angry with her."

"Nothing points to this being connected," Irene said through the ruined marshmallow in her mouth.

"We haven't found a note," I reminded Detective Price. "If someone was trying to threaten me, wouldn't they leave a note like they did before?"

He was thinking it through. I could tell by the way his fingers twisted that poor toasting stick. "If you all want to look at it from another perspective, it certainly couldn't hurt."

Piper nodded as if that was the reasonable reaction she'd expected.

It wasn't what I'd expected. I have no idea what I thought was going to happen, but I'd assumed it would be more . . . explosive than that.

Detective Price turned to me and gave me a grin that unsettled my belly—and not in a good way. "So. Let's talk about who might have it in for you. Do you have any enemies? Any business partners with a grudge, or angry ex-lovers?"

"Of course not." Why would someone be upset with me? I was a likable person.

Piper made a noise and everyone looked at her.

"You have something to add?" Detective Price asked.

"Maybe." Piper turned to me. "What about Morton?"

Nineteen

MY EX-BOYFRIEND'S NAME HUNG in the air between us all.

This would be a really good time for a fire sprite to reach up and pull the word into the flames.

"Who's Morton?" Detective Needs-To-Know-Everything asked.

"Her ex-boyfriend," Piper answered.

Now everyone was looking at me. I tried not to squirm. "Morton wouldn't do anything to hurt me."

"What about to scare you?" Irene asked. She reached out as if she could put her hand on my arm, but the fire was in the way. "None of this looks like it was meant to hurt. It looks like a warning—or a scare tactic."

"No. It wasn't Morton." I shook my head. It couldn't be him, and not just because I didn't want to believe someone who'd claimed to care about me would do this. "He's in Boston right now."

Detective Price's jaw tightened. He leaned

forward, resting his elbows on his knees. "Why do you know your ex-boyfriend's schedule? Are you trying to avoid him? Did he threaten you?"

"What? No." What was with these people? "Morton is a lovely person. He'd never do anything to hurt me. Or to scare me. I know where he is because that's where he's working right now. This is ridiculous."

Completely ridiculous, even if I could maybe, possibly, see Morton messing things up as a prank. Not to this extent, of course, but just enough to poke a little at my way of life.

I pushed to my feet and started gathering up my laundry so I'd be too busy to entertain that thought. A few of the tops could probably just have the soil and dust shaken off them, but some of the other things looked as if they'd been ground into the dirt. I'd definitely be doing laundry again in the morning, unless I just took care of it tonight.

With everything that had happened, there was a good chance I wouldn't be sleeping much. Who knew how long the detectives would hang around before giving up and leaving? Then I'd have to wind down before I could sleep, and it wasn't as if I'd be sleeping in. Frenzy would see to that, coming to beg for nuts.

Where had he gotten to, anyway? I looked into the trees. I needed to do something extra nice to thank him for alerting me to the intrusion.

"You called him her ex-boyfriend." Detective I-Don't-Care-If-I'm-Intruding's voice carried across to the deck where I was sorting through the clothes. "Were they together long? How long ago did they break up?"

"They were together off and on for a couple of years. I have no idea why it ended, or exactly when," Piper answered.

Of course she had no idea. I hadn't talked to her about it. She'd been traveling, and there'd been a lot to catch up on over the past couple of days.

"They were together when my husband and I left for our safari," Piper continued. "We don't normally go on long trips, but this was a gift from our parents for our anniversary. I didn't even know about the breakup until Morton canceled his performance with the symphony."

"He's a musician?" Irene asked.

Tired of them talking about it as if I couldn't hear them, I turned and went back to my spot by the fire. "He plays the French horn, but his career is as a conductor. He was supposed to conduct a concert here in a few days. Now he's not. End of story."

Detective Price's gaze flicked to me, so I knew he'd heard me, but he turned back to Piper. "When was your safari?"

"We were gone for six weeks, and we've been back a little over a week." Piper looked at me and shrugged. "I'm sorry, but you won't tell me about it. For all I know, he could have threatened you."

"He didn't threaten me." It might have been easier if he had. Then we could have all had a good laugh about it. "And I haven't told you about it because I haven't had a chance—there are always other people around. And with Ludwig dead, it feels like we have more important things to worry about than Morton."

Piper gave me a look that said she didn't believe me.

I shrugged. Just because it was the truth didn't mean I could make her believe it.

"We've taken enough of your night." Irene offered me a smile, then turned to Piper. "Come on. I'll give you a ride."

Piper wrapped her arms around me and squeezed tight. "Are you sure you'll be okay here?"

"Of course. Go home to your husband. Tell him I said thanks for letting me borrow you tonight."

They all headed down the drive to the vehicles, and I sat back down and stared into the fire.

Piper would probably follow me around with her violin, playing ear worms until I started talking. All it would take was one round of Pachelbel's Canon. I hated that almost as much as cellists did. Why did so many people like that piece? Almost every quartet gig wanted it played at some point. Didn't people realize they were just climbing on a very overused bandwagon?

Headlights flashed across the clearing as a black truck parked next to Betty. The rumble of the engine cut out and the lights turned off, then Detective Price climbed out of the cab. He closed the distance and sat beside me.

"You're back." Oh, how observant of me.

"I didn't mean to step on toes. If you say your ex didn't do this, I believe you." He offered up a real smile as a very persuasive peace offering. "I'm sure Detective Watson will still want to check his alibi, because she's thorough."

I dug a hole in the dirt using my big toe. "Morton and I broke up just after Piper left on her trip. It was my choice, not his."

"I don't need an explanation."

"I don't mind telling you." I was surprised when the words felt true. Maybe I'd been needing to talk about the whole thing and just hadn't realized it. "Telling Piper is hard. She was always happy that I had him. She didn't want me to be lonely."

Detective Price didn't take his eyes off the fire. "Were you lonely without him?"

"Of course not. I don't think I've ever been lonely, which is hard for someone like Piper to understand." There was always someone or something to step in and take my attention. And when there wasn't, I was perfectly happy with my own company. I'd always thought everyone felt the same, but then I met Piper and realized I was wrong. "Detective—"

"I'm off duty. Call me Jack." He half-turned toward me, giving me his full attention.

"Jack." Somehow, after hearing him say it, the name seemed to fit him better. Not perfectly, but better. "Do you get lonely?"

"Occasionally. My job comes with walls." Something unsettling flashed across his face. "Most people see me coming and get uncomfortable. They worry I'll find out about something they've done. It makes it hard to have friends."

I tried not to imagine him sitting home at night because people were wary of cops. "Why would people care if you know what they've done?"

"Not everyone is as comfortable with who they are as you seem to be."

I laughed. "Most people aren't comfortable with who I am. I have to accept myself, because there's no guarantee anyone else will."

The fire snapped as a log shifted, sending a trail of sparks into the air.

Jack shifted beside me.

Had he moved closer to me? It was hard to tell, but I almost thought he had.

Maybe he felt the same draw I felt, or the thickness in the air between us.

He looked at me as if my thoughts were written out across my face, then ran his hands down his thighs. "It's late and you've had an eventful day. You must be tired."

I adjusted my glasses as I looked away. "Thank you for coming to make sure things were okay."

Jack set his hand on my shoulder, sending ripples of . . . *something* through me. "I'll keep an eye on things for what's left of the night. Sleep well, Octavia. You're safe."

I hurried inside, away from whatever was

happening between us that Jack didn't want to acknowledge.

Up in my sleeping loft, I peeked out the window as Jack added a log to the fire.

Knowing he was there, that he would keep me safe, touched something deep inside me. And, surprisingly, I slept.

Twenty

"I'M NOT COMFORTABLE WITH YOU being alone until we have this case wrapped up," Jack said through the clothespins in his mouth. He pulled one free and used it to secure the shoulder of a blouse to the cord stretching between trees. Then he repeated the process with the other one.

Who'd have thought the man would know his way around a clothesline?

Of course I was surprised. I bet you don't know what to do with one. Okay, maybe you do. But most people these days would rather toss their laundry in a machine instead of letting the fresh air dry them.

I set down the almost-empty basket. "I'll be fine."

He reached for my favorite worn shorts and secured them to the line next to the blouse. "When you're here alone, lock your door."

"That might be a little hard. I don't have a lock."

"You don't have a lock." He looked like he

wanted to say more about that, then changed his mind. "I'll keep watch at night. At least for today, I can't spare anyone from my team to stay with you. I've asked Hector to keep an eye on you."

"Hector already has a security job. I've lived this long without a babysitter. I'll be fine." As I spoke, I fished a pair of long striped socks out of the bottom of the basket and hung them to dry.

Detective Bossy-Pants picked up the empty basket. "Stop being stubborn, Octavia. I need to solve Ludwig's murder, and worrying about your safety will split my focus."

Well, we couldn't have that, could we? Not a split focus.

All the happy feelings toward the man that I'd been swimming in since he showed up, off duty and ready to protect, disappeared as if a switch had flipped.

I yanked the basket out of his hands and headed toward the house. "I'm fine. Go to work. Save the day."

"Wait. What just happened?"

In the reflection of a window I saw him staring after me, hands on his hips and looking completely baffled.

I was baffled, too, under the sudden anger. I always allowed myself to accept whatever feelings I had, but they never changed that quickly.

It was a new experience, and entirely unnerving.

Suddenly needing to get away from whatever all this was, I set the basket on the deck, then went over and climbed into Betty. Sure, Piper had said she'd come get me since I'd left Clover at the shop, but I didn't feel like waiting.

"Where are you going?" Jack called out as his long legs ate up the distance between us.

"I have a job to get to," I answered, turning the key. Betty spluttered to life.

"You can't—We weren't done talking." He shook his head, then pulled his keys out of his pocket. "At least let me give you a ride."

I shifted Betty into gear and pulled away.

So, I feel like I should probably point out right about now that I don't lose my temper very often.

I don't usually even get angry. Going with the flow had been part of me for so long it was as natural as breathing.

But between the stress of the past few days, the extra short night of sleep, and the overbearing detective who was distinctly talented at finding buttons I didn't even know I had and pushing them as hard as he could, I wasn't exactly feeling zen.

When his truck turned onto the road behind me, I almost decided to pass Aerie Pines and see how long he'd tail me. How's that for splitting his focus?

But, because I knew Piper would end up wasting her morning looking for me, I turned into the parking lot.

I chose an out-of-the-way parking spot and tucked the key back under the visor before hopping out.

Detective Let-Me-Focus had parked closer, so I couldn't slip past him.

That didn't mean I couldn't try.

I put on a burst of speed, ignoring the little piece of gravel digging deeper into the bottom of my foot every time I stepped on it.

Detective Price grabbed my shoulders as I tried to sprint past and spun me so I was facing him. "What has gotten into you? You ran off in the middle of a conversation."

"I drove off," I corrected. "And the conversation was over. Just like it is now."

His arms fell to his side.

"Well, well, what do we have here?" Piper's voice cut in. She joined us, her eyes drifting down Detective Price's rumpled hair.

He looked good rumpled, which just annoyed me even more, especially since my fingers in his hair hadn't been what rumpled him.

"We're fine," Jack and I said at the same time.

"Clearly," Piper said.

I tried not to smile as I looked at Jack, feeling a sudden shift in the air as we went from verbal opponents to siding together against Piper. His face was free of expression, but his eyes twinkled.

Piper decided to try again. "Octavia, you were yelling."

I shrugged. "I need to get to work."

"Stay in the shop with the door locked—you do have a lock on that door, don't you?—until Hector gets there. I mean it. Don't put even one of those bare toes out the door." Jack's voice promised we'd continue whatever it was Piper had interrupted.

For two seconds, we'd been on the same side. The two of us against Piper. Then he had to go and ruin it by ordering me around again. Confused by the abrupt, unexpected changes in tempo, I turned and walked away.

"What did you do to her?" Piper's voice demanded behind me.

I slowed down a little so I wouldn't miss the answer.

"She got upset with me. I have no idea why."

Ha! If he didn't know, I'd have to enlighten him. If I ever figured it out myself.

"Octavia doesn't get upset. Ever." Then Piper gasped. "You broke her."

Their voices were far enough behind me that I missed whatever came next.

I followed the path toward my shop, trying to shake the strong emotions Jack had created.

Yes, of course I had a lock on the shop door. What did the man take me for? I wasn't entirely naïve. Besides, the shop's insurance required it. Since I needed insurance to qualify to run the place—not to mention, the building I rented came with one—it wasn't something I'd even thought about.

And why did it matter if I was alone? I spent most of my time in my own company. I was willing to bet in his role as a detective, Jack didn't go out of his way to get security for people on the edges of his investigations, especially when they didn't qualify for a police officer to do the protecting.

Shaking the thoughts free, I unlocked the shop and stepped inside, letting the door swing closed behind me. I hesitated, then flicked the lock, telling myself it wasn't because Jack had told me to.

Two minutes later when I was unlocking the door for Piper, I wondered why I'd bothered in the first place.

Piper flounced in and pointed to the lock.

I rolled my eyes as I relocked it. "Happy now?"

"You know, I think I am." She swung her hips. "Someone made you lose control. And not just any someone."

There was another tap on the door.

Piper pouted. "I wanted to talk with you before Hector got here."

I opened the door. "Good morning, Hector. You really don't need to do this."

"I have my orders," he said. Then he nodded at Piper.

Piper fluttered her eyelashes in response. "I should get home and have breakfast before rehearsal. I'll be back this afternoon, Octavia. I want to hear all about your night."

Unlike a certain detective I could name, Hector was happy to blend into the background. He pulled a chair out of the office and sat in the corner of the shop, keeping an eye on things while I went about my day.

And something about that made me angry all

over again.

Not at Hector. No, Hector was the epitome of professional.

I was upset with Jack. Or maybe it was Detective Price.

Yes, I do realize they're the same person. But at the same time, they're not. Detective Price was the bossy professional persona. Jack was sweet and a little vulnerable.

Which one was responsible for giving me a babysitter for the second day in a row?

Which one had made the choice to spend the night outside so I could sleep?

And which one had decided to announce he'd be sitting outside my house again tonight, whether I asked for it or not?

This wasn't a good idea. No, not because I might decide to yank him inside to see if we could have another moment or twenty. Because having the lead detective on a murder investigation giving up his sleep meant the person in charge would be playing with half an instrument instead of a full section.

That wasn't going to happen because of me. Ludwig deserved justice. Cora and the kids deserved justice.

Heck, even the symphony deserved justice.

That meant someone was going to have to solve the case, and if Jack was too busy splitting his focus and making himself tired, someone else was going to to have to help.

Twenty-One

I LOCKED MYSELF IN THE shop's office—see? The shop had more than one lock—then went over and opened the window. A smattering of wildflowers under the window swayed to music I couldn't hear. I pushed myself through the opening, carefully lowering myself to the ground.

Ducking low, I crept along the back of the building, passing under the windows to make sure Eli and Jamie wouldn't see me and rat me out to Hector.

Now, don't you start on me. I know Hector was there for my safety. But Tatiana was enough of a snob that she wouldn't want to talk to me if I brought along security.

Oh, right. I hadn't told you I was heading over to see Tatiana. My bad.

Let's try this again.

After deciding someone had to take the investigation into their own hands—yes, that was me and my hands—I had to figure out where to start.

I saw two possible courses of action. I could go talk to Vanessa again, or I could question Tatiana.

Since Irene and I had made an impromptu visit to the housing office already, and since my home was ransacked within a few hours of that, I decided it might be safer to start with Tatiana.

See? I was being careful enough that even Detective Price couldn't say I was being reckless, and since he seemed to think breathing was reckless, that was saying something.

Maybe I was still a little grumpy.

I made it away from the shop and into the grove of pine trees that almost met the building without getting caught. Instead of heading to the path, which Hector could easily see through the window if he turned his head, I cut through the trees, kicking up the familiar scent of the woods. I came out the other side on the path heading up toward the apartments.

I passed the first set of buildings—three unimaginative, but nice, rectangles that formed a square with the path as the final side—and went to the second, identical grouping. Tatiana always stayed on the end apartment of the top floor of that center building, looking out at the tree-topped cliff.

As I made my way up to her door, I started having second thoughts about the whole thing.

Did I expect to learn things the detectives couldn't? Of course not. But I hoped I might help speed things along.

That's the story I was telling myself, anyway. It sounded better than the one where I decided to poke around a murder investigation just to spite the lead detective on the case.

I brushed the thought aside. As long as I didn't run into Piper, or anyone who might talk to Piper, I'd be fine. No one would have to find out I was taking things into my own hands—which were pretty capable, if I say so myself. I'd like to see Detective This-Is-My-Investigation try to play the Rebecca Clark Sonata. Ha!

I stood in front of Tatiana's door. Was it a bad idea to come here without telling anyone where I'd gone? Probably. I shrugged to myself. It was too late to do anything about it now. I knocked.

The door swung open.

Tatiana's smile disappeared. "Oh. It's you."

"Can I talk to you for a minute?" I asked. Hopefully politeness would win out. "Please."

She stepped back just far enough to let me squeeze past her into the living area.

I glanced around, surprised by the deep red walls that would have looked at home next to my gypsy caravan.

Tatiana closed the door. "Can I get you a drink?"

I shook my head. "I'm fine, thank you."

"You might as well sit down." She took her own advice and dropped onto a fainting couch that had to be antique.

I sat on her fainting couch's twin and ran my hand across the soft fabric. Furniture like that made me want to reconsider my lifestyle. I didn't just love the fainting couch, I coveted it. "I won't take a lot of your time."

"You're just following up on rumors, I know." The fingers of her left hand twitched against her thumb, making me wonder what music she was playing in her head.

What kind of a soundtrack would Tatiana live to? Something flashy. Based on her living room, I'd say it was probably traditional. Weiniawski, or Sarasate? Or maybe Paganini.

I shook my head. This wasn't the time to get sidetracked. "You told me you were planning to meet with the board, but you already had."

She huffed. "So?"

It was probably better to ease into it. "What did they tell you?"

She gave me one of the looks she seemed to reserve just for me. "If you didn't know what they said, you wouldn't be here."

Well, she had me there.

"You don't like me, I don't like you, so why don't we cut to the chase?" Tatiana leaned forward, and her fingers stopped playing whatever they'd been practicing. "Tell me what you know, and I'll fill in the blanks. Then you can cross me off your little suspect list and let me get on with my day."

"They told you they wouldn't fire Ludwig," I blurted, thinking over what Piper had shared.

She nodded. "Next."

"Actually, what I heard was that the only way

Ludwig was leaving was if he chose to go." Which didn't make sense. Everyone was supposed to go through the blind audition at the end of the contract term.

"You see it, don't you?" Tatiana pulled her feet up beside her. In anyone else it would have looked like they were making themselves smaller. With Tatiana, it only made her look more in charge. "You're annoying, but you aren't stupid. And if the two of us see it, surely someone else did, too."

"Who else would know they weren't going to make Ludwig jump through hoops to re-up his contract?"

"That's the real question, isn't it? Find that person, and you'll have your killer."

It made a surprising amount of sense, for Tatiana.

On the other hand, it's not something I'd even considered up to this point, and I'd gotten two threats already, if you counted the strange mess at my house as a threat. And maybe hanging around detectives was rubbing off on me, but I was starting to think they were right about that.

We already knew the mess hadn't been caused by Morton. And pretending it might have been animals, or a lost hiker, was almost as ridiculous as the Morton idea.

So, would a killer wait until you were looking in their direction before warning you off, or send you a warning before they were on your radar?

That depended on the killer, didn't it?

"I suppose that depends on if they had a reason for not making Ludwig reaudition," I said. It was possible. Maybe not probable, but possible. "Could they have given him a longer contract to begin with? Part of taking the job as concertmaster, maybe."

Tatiana's smug smile was back in place. "I'd say it was possible, except that one of the board members let it slip."

I wasn't sure I wanted to know how Tatiana had gotten the board member to let it slip. There wasn't much I'd put past her. "Okay. That throws a new spin on things. I'll have to look into that. But, while I'm here, I have to ask."

She waved her hand between us, inviting me to do my worst.

"How upset were you when you left that meeting?"

She didn't even hesitate before answering. "If Ludwig had been in the hallway, I'd have taken a good swing at him. We all worked hard to get where we are. I deserved the chance the blind audition would have given me. I'm a better musician than he is. Piper's a better musician than him. Almost every violinist in that symphony plays better than he does."

"You think you deserve his seat?" I hadn't meant to ask the question. It just shot out of me.

"I would do a much better job than he ever did. I know the music. I know how to lead. People like me more than him." She paused and inclined her head toward me. "Present company excluded."

I'd been out of the symphony too long to know how true that was. But from what I'd gleaned from my place behind the speaker stands, I'd say she was at least mostly right.

"So, you want to know, did I kill him? The answer is no. I didn't. Not because I didn't want to. I did. Someone else got to him first."

Twenty-Two

I WAS STILL THINKING ABOUT Tatiana as I climbed back through the window into the violin shop office. For what might be the first time ever, I believed her.

Not because she was polite, or because she did her best to answer my questions.

No, I believed her because she told me she'd wanted to kill Ludwig.

Does that seem backwards? Maybe a confession like that should have me looking at her more closely. But the look on her face when she said someone had gotten to him first had been very convincing.

I pushed my glasses up my nose and glanced in the mirror Mairi had insisted belonged in the office so we could make sure we were presentable.

My reflection suggested Mairi's comment might have been about all of us, but was likely pointed at me.

I pulled pine needles from my fuzzy hair and

twisted it into a braid, then straightened my top. I couldn't do anything about my dirty feet without water, but no one was likely to think it was out of place.

There was a knock on the door, and the doorknob rattled. "Octavia?"

I opened the door and Piper breezed through. "There you are. Did you fall asleep at the desk? I've knocked every few minutes for the past half hour."

Instead of answering the question, I deflected. "Last night wore me out."

She took the bait. "Did Jack figure out who caused the problems?"

I shook my head, feeling a little sorry about keeping secrets from her. But if she knew I'd climbed out the window to avoid my security guard, she'd be siding with the man who'd put me under surveillance in the first place.

"Are you sure it wasn't Morton?" she asked.

"Of course I am." She was never going to let it go, was she?

She sat in the desk chair that I'd been supposedly sleeping in. "It's time, Octavia. What happened between you and Morton?"

I glanced at the closed door. We finally had time, just the two of us. And since I'd almost told Jack—who was basically a stranger—about the breakup, I should be able to confide in my best friend.

I took a deep breath. "We ended it just after you went on your trip."

"Why? You were perfect together."

"You've said that from the day we met. Would you even see it if we were all wrong for each other?"

There was a shuffling outside the door. "Speak up, we can't hear you," Xavier said.

"Go back to work," I hollered. Then I got up and locked the door for good measure.

Piper's brow was furrowed as she gave my question real consideration. "You seemed happy together. Was I just imagining that?"

"No, we were fine." I sat on the couch and scrubbed my face with my hands. "We were fine."

"Fine isn't a good word when you're describing a relationship."

"We had some fun," I admitted. When he'd been willing to take breaks from his job and meet me on the road, wherever I happened to be at the time, we'd share the adventure of living. We'd explored some of the most out-of-the-way corners of the country together, and enjoyed it.

"So what happened?" Piper asked again.

I moaned.

"You'll feel better once you've told me."

She was right, of course.

But—

Okay.

Here goes.

"He wanted to get married."

Stop laughing. Seriously, I can totally hear you. Okay, I can't, but I can sure imagine it.

I'm going to pretend you aren't listening. Just— don't do anything to bring attention to yourself, okay?

Piper was struggling to keep a straight face.

I bit my lip. This was why I'd been worried about telling her. Piper was Marriage Material. She always had been. She was probably thinking about how most people would be excited to get a proposal.

She started to giggle, then it turned into a full belly laugh. She grabbed for a tissue and dabbed at her eyes. When she finally got herself under control, she just shook her head at me. "Doesn't the man know you at all?"

I couldn't have heard her right. "What?"

"Come on, Octavia. Everyone knows you're not the kind of person to settle down." She waved her tissue in the air. "Morton absolutely knows it. Isn't that why you've taken so many breaks from each other? He wanted you to stay with him instead of heading out on another adventure?"

She'd noticed.

Still, she'd thought we were perfect together, which was obviously wrong, so I wasn't sure I should trust her judgment completely.

"Where were you? Did he have a ring? What exactly did he say?" Piper asked. "I have to picture the whole thing so I know how hard to laugh in his face the next time I run into him."

There was a reason Piper was my best friend. Even when my decisions were the exact opposite of what she would choose, she had my back. "He had a ring. A diamond big enough to feed an entire village for a year."

"That was his first—well, not his first mistake. But a big one. He should have spent the money to *actually* feed a village if he wanted your attention." Piper looked at the diamond sitting on her own finger. "I love my sparkles, but you're more of a hemp bracelet and change the world kind of woman."

I felt lighter than I had in a while. It was nice when someone understood you. "He wanted me to sell the tiny house, and Betty. He suggested Clover could use a makeover."

"What, did he expect you to move into the suburbs?"

"Not the suburbs. A house in the city, near the university." I started laughing at the memory. "He said he needed me to stay there with him and support his career. Host dinner parties for his professor friends. And maybe, when there were school breaks, we could go on vacations so I wouldn't want to take off when he needed me there."

Piper took a few seconds to lift her jaw off the floor. "And what were you supposed to get from all this?"

"Stability." The word tasted nasty. Who needed stability? Not me. I'd never wanted to keep the status quo.

Then again, as Morton had gone out of his way to remind me, I wasn't normal.

Piper snorted. "Stability. The man doesn't have any idea who you are, does he? He just wants to put you in his little box. You know what? You're right. That scene last night couldn't have been Morton. He doesn't have enough imagination to cross the country and scatter laundry. If he was trying to get back at you, he'd just show up and propose again."

I laughed again.

"Oooo. We should call him and tell him all the reasons it wouldn't work between you." Piper's eyes were sparkling again, which meant I needed to stop her before she reached for her phone.

"I'd rather just leave things alone. It's been weeks now, and I haven't heard from him. Let's not break the trend."

Her face fell, but not for long. "I bet that's why he backed out of the concert. He was afraid we'd gang up on him."

It was a definite possibility. Apparently he'd never quite grasped the fact that I wasn't looking for anything serious. I just wanted a little fun.

And, strangely, the man who'd embraced the living for appearances thing had started out looking for fun, too.

I must have been his wild oats.

Well, the joke was on him. Because I still got to be wild. Still got to have fun. I didn't need him to make life interesting. I'd had plenty of fun when he'd taken breaks from our relationship to go remind himself what shape his mold was supposed to be.

Piper picked a pine needle off the desk. "Now, how about you tell me the real reason you weren't answering the door?"

Twenty-Three

THE REST OF THE DAY passed without incident, unless you counted Xavier pestering me about all the details he missed when he had his ear pressed against the office door.

Just as we were getting ready to close, Detective Price came in. He'd taken the time to change into a suit. There were shadows under his eyes, and he looked relaxed, but other than that he looked the same as he had the first time I'd seen him.

He looked toward Hector, who nodded but didn't move from his chair, then crossed to where I was closing out the till for the day. "Thank you for staying safe today. I get the feeling being asked to stay put for a day isn't the easiest thing for you."

I bit my lip to stop myself from blurting out the fact that I hadn't exactly stayed put.

"Please say she can stay out of the shop and roam around all day tomorrow." Xavier dropped to his knees to add more drama to his begging. "Or for a week, or even the whole summer."

Jack took my elbow and led me outside where Xavier couldn't interrupt as easily.

The breeze felt wonderful after spending most of the day indoors.

Xavier pressed his face to the glass as if that would let him be part of whatever was about to happen. It was only when Mairi rubbed glass cleaner on his face trying to get rid of his nose print that he gave up.

I understood. My curiosity was close to the breaking point, too. "What's going on?"

"We've taken Vanessa Chambers in for questioning. Detective Locke just left with her."

"What?" I felt like a percussionist had smashed my head between his cymbals. I hadn't even gotten a chance to talk to her again.

"The information she gave you and Detective Watson yesterday was enough to warrant some digging."

"You did enough digging in one day to label her a murderer? Murderess? Killer?" My mind spun. My little bit of investigating had been pointless.

"We don't know anything for sure about that, but it fits."

I thought detectives were supposed to gather the facts and let those tell them what happened, not try to fit the facts with a theory.

He glanced at something on his phone, then tucked it into his pocket and turned the full force of his attention on me. "We looked into her financials. She's been taking bribes from people to make housing arrangements in their favor."

I wanted to say that didn't sound like a big deal, but that was clearly not the reaction I was supposed to give. But I wasn't about to condemn the woman for trying to make a little extra dough. In an effort to be diplomatic, I didn't say anything.

"We'll be able to hold her on the bribes while we look into whether or not she tracked down the victim and killed him." Detective Price took a step closer. "I'm still planning to come over tonight so you can sleep easy, but I'll be late. I stopped by your place on my way here and everything looked the same as we left it. Just as a precaution, I'm going to stop again on my way out."

That didn't make sense. "I thought you had your suspect in custody."

"We might, but until I know that for sure I'm not taking any chances with your safety." He bent down until his face was right in front of mine. "Is there anyone you trust to watch your back until I can get there tonight?"

I tried not to lean into his closeness. "Don't worry about me. Do what you have to do, then go home and get some sleep. I'll stay with Piper tonight."

"I'm not trying to run you out of your home."

I grabbed at my hair—the braid had come out hours ago—and tossed it over my shoulder. "I'm not running."

He watched me for a while, then nodded. "I

need to get going. I'll check on you in the morning."

As I watched him stride away, I almost changed my mind and asked him to come back after his interrogation.

When he was out of sight, I went back into the shop Mairi and Xavier were busy cleaning up, so I managed to avoid their—and by their, I mean Xavier's—constant need for gossip.

I thanked Hector profusely and sent him off to either go home or do the work he should have been doing instead of babysitting me, then I slipped out and grabbed Clover.

I might be too late to ask Vanessa about anything, but she wasn't the only one who worked in the housing office. Maybe Tammy Spencer knew more than she was telling.

As I pedaled closer, I saw extra activity around the administration buildings. Now that Detective Price's team was on their way out, everyone was standing around talking about what had happened.

I stopped and leaned Clover against the building, then started wandering through the group looking for Tammy.

Ideas and questions about why Vanessa had been taken in bounced around. No one said anything about bribes, but lots of people were jumping to the conclusion that she had something to do with Ludwig's death.

Which, to be fair, she might have.

Finally, on the other side of the crowd, I saw Tammy's pale hair. I wound my way over to her.

She saw me coming and stiffened.

"Tammy, wait," I called.

She glanced around. Maybe she decided it would be better to get our conversation over with, or maybe she decided it was safer to talk to me with all these witnesses. Either way, she stopped.

I went up to her, ready to charm her into telling me everything she knew. "Are you okay?"

"What do you want?"

Okay, so maybe I wasn't very good at charming people. I should have brought Piper with me. She could get people to pour their hearts out without even realizing it. "I just wanted to get your opinion on something Vanessa told me yesterday. You remember I came and talked to her at the end of the day?"

"As if I could forget," Tammy muttered. "You keep poking your nose in."

That was certainly true. It wasn't something I was used to doing. "I'm sorry. I don't mean to be a nuisance."

"Fine. I'll give you two minutes." She tugged at the hem of her T-shirt, then moved farther away from the general gossipers.

Now that I was faced with a time limit, all my questions disappeared.

It was like that dream. No, not that one. The one where you're playing the biggest performance of your life, and not only do you forget the notes, but you completely forget how to play music.

What, you don't have that dream?

Well, what does your subconscious obsess over instead?

The snapping of fingers in my face brought me back. "Time's ticking. You said something about what Vanessa told you yesterday?"

"Right. Um. She said she went looking for Ludwig just before he died."

"Oh, that. Yeah, never mind that."

"What?"

"Yeah. I thought she might have killed Mr. Baylor. But she couldn't have. She was in the hotel." Tammy looked over my shoulder. "Is that all?"

I started to ask if she knew anything about the bribes, but she darted around me and hurried over to one of the groundskeepers who was just joining the group. From the way she wrapped herself around him, she wouldn't notice if Detective Price showed back up and announced Vanessa was guilty of it all.

"There you are," Piper cried as she ran up to me. She took in the scene. "I've heard so many rumors, but Xavier said Jack came and talked to you privately about whatever's going on. What do you know?"

Jack hadn't said I should keep it a secret, but he hadn't said I shouldn't, either. The conversation had felt private, after he'd dragged me out of the shop.

But I trusted Piper.

But I also knew she put the tabloids to shame in her thirst for gossip.

Okay, so maybe I kept our conversation to myself, but shared what I knew about Vanessa looking for Ludwig. Or had I already told her that?

"Stop thinking so hard and talk," Piper said.

I backed away from the crowd. When you were surrounded by musicians, you had to beware of keen ears. When we were far enough away I deemed it safe to talk, I told her about Vanessa looking for Ludwig, and how Tammy said Vanessa couldn't have killed him because she was in the hotel when he died.

Piper's excitement grew until she almost exploded. "That's easy enough to check. All we have to do is check the security footage."

"I'm sure Detective Price already took that."

"Why aren't you calling him Jack?" she asked.

That was a loaded question, especially since she'd gone out of her way to sound all innocent.

Listen, I know Piper better than almost anyone, and when she takes that tone it's because she's trying to trick you into telling her something she doesn't think you'd share willingly.

If she ever talks to you like that and you don't know exactly what you're doing, you're better off running the other direction.

Luckily, my years as her best friend had given me so many chances to practice at it that I'd gotten almost as good at dealing with that fake innocence as I was at playing the viola.

Even with all that experience, I chose my words carefully. "We're talking about something he would have done in his role as a detective. So it makes sense to use his title right now."

"So if I were to ask what happened between the two of you after Irene and I left last night, then you'd be talking about Jack?" Her innocent tone hadn't left. If anything, it had intensified.

I decided to sidestep the question. "Focus, Piper. How are we going to see the footage if it's already being logged in as evidence?"

"Come on." She dove into the crowd, holding onto my arm so she wouldn't lose me as she made her way to the winding path through a stand of trees to the back patio of the hotel.

As we left the trees, she finally slowed down. "When we get inside, let me do the talking."

I was fine with that. I didn't know what we were doing.

Piper walked into the employee area as if she had every right to be there. She stopped outside a door and knocked.

The door swung open, and a wiry man with a long nose popped his head into the hallway. "Piper Holland. I was wondering when you were going to stop by. Come in."

Piper dragged me into a small, semi-dark room. One wall was covered in camera feeds from the common areas of the hotel. "I need a favor."

The man laughed. "Of course you do. What is it?"

"You've heard about the murder at the amphitheater, of course." Piper leaned close to him and fluttered her eyelashes. "My friend and I need to see your footage from the time leading up to that."

He looked around as if he expected someone to be watching. "What?"

"The security footage. Please."

"The detectives took all that right after it happened." He pulled a face at her and shook his head.

She pulled back. "Of course they did. Well, I suppose you can't share what you don't have."

I stepped toward the door.

"Um. Hold on." He turned to a machine and did something I couldn't make out. "At least let me get you a drink, since you came all the way over here to visit. I'll be right back."

As he scurried out the door, Piper dragged me over to the monitors. "This is your one chance. Don't miss anything," she hissed in my ear.

The date and time stamp in the corner of every screen showed this was the footage that was supposed to be with the detectives.

Instead of asking questions I knew would go unanswered, I watched the screens.

I pointed to the view of the back doors that Piper and I had just come through as it showed Vanessa arriving. I grabbed a paper off the desk and wrote down the time, then wrote down everything she did, along with the times. When she finally went back out the door she'd entered, I looked at my list.

Tammy was right. Vanessa had been inside the hotel from the time Ludwig left my shop until just before I found him.

She was innocent.

Twenty-Four

TWO DAYS LATER, VERY LITTLE had changed.

Vanessa had been arrested for taking bribes. Detective Price was less than appreciative when I'd had Piper call and tell him we'd found her alibi for the murder, but it had officially checked out.

And I was officially out of suspects. What did the detectives know that I didn't? Because they were sure keeping busy.

Jack kept checking up on me, but didn't have time to stick around and make sure I was safe at night. Which was fine.

Okay, it wasn't fine. I'd thought that even though there wasn't anything romantic starting up between us, we were at least becoming friends. But dangle a murder investigation in front of the guy, and he'll forget all about his budding friendships.

I was starting to understand why he said it was hard for him to have friends. It wasn't about walls. It was that you have to be a friend to have one.

The important thing, though, was that I hadn't received any more threats.

That's why it was such a surprise when I almost ran straight into the front of Jack's trying-too-hard-to-be-overlooked truck when I was steering Clover out to the road and Jack was turning in. I braked hard, skidding through the gravel.

When he climbed out, it was obvious this was Detective Price, not just Jack. He was in one of those suits that hugged his broad shoulders just right while announcing that no one else on earth was as put together as he was. But it was his no-nonsense expression that drove it all home.

And he didn't even ask if I was okay after he'd almost run me down at the mouth of my own driveway.

Well, my grandmother's driveway, but it was mine for the summer.

He reached for my bike, barely letting me scramble off it and grab the bag from Clover's basket before he lifted it in the air and loaded it in the back of his truck. Then he opened the passenger door. "Get in."

I planted my feet and crossed my arms. "I haven't done anything wrong this time."

He closed his eyes and sighed. "I'm running on four hours of sleep in the past week, I've had amateurs poking around in my investigation, and I haven't eaten in fourteen hours. I'm going the same place you are, which means it makes sense to give you a ride. Could you please just get in and let me do one nice thing today before I have to be hard?"

It wasn't his confession of having a hard week that had me scurrying over to hop inside. It wasn't even his use of the word *please*.

Mostly, it was because he was making time to be nice. But also, his face was changing color again. That shade of red didn't look good on anyone. If getting into his giant truck would keep him from giving himself a stroke, I'd do it.

Because that's what friends do.

When he climbed in behind the wheel, I handed him a jar I'd pulled out of my little patchwork backpack. I'd planned to have it for breakfast when I got to Aerie Pines, but since I'd already eaten a handful of the nuts I kept on hand for Frenzy, I was in better shape than Jack was. "Eat."

He looked in the jar as if he didn't recognize food. "What is it?"

"My homemade granola and yogurt."

At first it looked like he wasn't going to even try it. Then he screwed the top off the jar and sniffed.

"It's good for you," I assured him. "Oh, wait, let me get you a spoon."

He rolled his eyes at the set of travel cutlery. "You carry the strangest things."

I didn't usually even carry a bag. He just happened to catch me on an off day.

Jack poked at the granola with the spoon a few times as if he really couldn't believe anyone would eat this kind of thing, then took a bite. Soon he was scraping the bottom of the jar. By the time he screwed the lid back into place, his color was back to normal and the grump lines between his brows had smoothed out. "Thanks."

"You're welcome." I took the jar and tucked it back into the bag. "Why are you headed to Aerie Pines so early today?"

His face closed off. "I need to talk to a suspect."

"You have a suspect? Who is it?" I sat up taller. "I thought we were out of suspects."

"You're staying out of this, remember?"

That's what he thought. We'd come this far together—well, maybe not *together*, but at least alongside each other—that he couldn't really believe he was going to keep me out of it now, could he?

Well, Detective Has-To-Solve-It-On-His-Own had better think again.

"I shouldn't have said as much as I did." He put the truck into gear and pulled onto the road.

Because he looked so tired—and I was still a little concerned his face might go all red again and he'd collapse and I'd have to steal his phone and brave a call for an ambulance—I didn't reply.

When we got to Aerie Pines, Irene and Detective Locke were waiting in the parking lot. They stood off to the side while Jack retrieved Clover.

Jack wheeled the bike to me and tipped the handlebars my direction. "Go right to your shop."

"Can you at least give me a hint about your suspect?"

"No." He started to walk toward the other detectives.

I fell into step beside him. "Do I know them? What questions are you going to ask? What makes them a suspect? Do they know you're coming, or are you surprising them?"

Irene and Detective Locke overheard my stream of questions as we got closer. They weren't quite as good at hiding their emotions as Jack was, so their lips were twitching.

"You don't need to know any of that," Jack growled.

Maybe I should have fed him more than granola and yogurt when he showed up all grouchy and nearly ran me over. I reached into my bag, then passed him the candy bar I'd planned to give Piper. "Here. I think you need this."

He looked at the fair trade label as if it wasn't written in English. "What?"

"Clearly the granola didn't fix you, but good chocolate fixes everything." I rang Clover's bell for emphasis.

"She has a point," Irene choked out while pretending she wasn't laughing. "Eat the chocolate. It's good for you."

"That's what she said about the granola," he muttered, but he unwrapped a corner of the candy bar, took a bite, and swallowed hard.

He didn't even take the time to savor it. I know! What kind of monster does that? He needed to mellow out enough to taste it. That chocolate had come halfway around the world to tease his tastebuds. "What are you doing?"

"I'm eating the chocolate, just like I've been ordered to do." He didn't sound like someone who'd just eaten good chocolate. It was supposed to make him happy, not annoyed.

Detective Locke cleared his throat. "As entertaining as all this is, we have someone to interview."

"*Who?*" I demanded. "Why? What do you know?"

"One of the reports came in," Irene said.

Jack tried to stop her, but ended up choking on a bite of chocolate instead.

Serves him right for not taking the time to let it melt on his tongue.

Irene ignored his obvious displeasure in sharing anything with me. "There was DNA under the victim's fingernails. It matched DNA we had on file."

I felt like I'd taken a wrong step and fallen off the stage in the middle of a performance. "You had someone's DNA on file? Someone that works *here*? Whose? Why?"

"It's not the first time she's been suspected of something serious. She was almost deported a few years ago."

Deported? There were lots of amazing people here who hadn't started out their lives as American citizens, but only one not so amazing person—at least when it came to me—that had been on my own very short list. "You can't mean Tatiana."

Jack recovered from his coughing fit to glare at Irene. "Now you've done it."

Twenty-Five

"BUT I TALKED TO TATIANA. She was meeting with the board when Ludwig died." I had to rush to keep up with Jack's long strides.

Amazingly, the other detectives didn't have the same trouble.

Jack stopped and turned to glare at me. "You did what? When? You were supposed to be staying out of things."

Huh. The chocolate really hadn't worked. That had to be a first.

His face was getting redder by the second. That wasn't a first, which bothered me more than it should.

"If we're going to get there before the rehearsal starts, we don't really have time for this," Detective Locke said. He gave me an encouraging smile as Detective Leave-My-Investigation-Alone turned and stalked toward the amphitheater.

"For your information, the board meeting was over before he died," he ground out. "She had opportunity and motive. She has access to, and is presumably strong enough to lift that statue. That gives her means."

How did he manage to talk with his jaw so tight? I wouldn't have thought it was physically possible. And didn't those tense muscles hurt? Not to mention what it was doing to his aura.

Before I could think of anything to say to that, we got to the amphitheater and Jack was hopping onto the stage where half the symphony members were warming up before their rehearsal for the evening's 1812 Overture concert.

I leaned Clover against the nearest chairs and hurried up after him.

Donning the full mantle of his title, Detective Price caught Tatiana's eye and motioned her over to the edge of the stage.

She hung her violin on the lip of the music stand, placing her bow across it, and joined us. If she was surprised to see me with the team of detectives, she didn't show it. "Rehearsal will be starting soon. What can't wait?"

Detective Price stared her down. "It might help if you remember we're investigating the murder of one of your colleagues."

Tatiana's hand cut through the air. "Well?"

"Please go over your movements of that morning for me again." Detective Price pulled a notebook from his pocket, flipped it open, and ran a finger down the page.

From my vantage point near his elbow, I could

see the notebook page was blank. It was all for show.

Detective Price pressed on. "Specifically, what did you do between the rehearsal and when the body was found?"

"I met with the board. I've told you this already." Her fingers started tapping against the cushion of her thumb, running through the notes of something only she could hear.

"Funny thing," Detective Watson said. I couldn't call her by her first name at this point, either. She looked way too much like a cop right now. "The board members said you only stayed for a few minutes. Since their meeting was over before the victim was found, you have a significant gap in your alibi. So tell us, where did you go after you left that meeting?"

As the conversation had progressed, the musicians nearest us—the back half of the violin sections—had stopped warming up to listen. The quiet had worked across the symphony until even the people on the other side of the stage were trying to hear.

Tatiana's eyes cut to me. "You had to keep pushing, didn't you?"

"What did you do?" Detective Price asked.

She kept talking at me. "He didn't deserve it. The chair, the good violin, any of it. The only reason he had it all was because he had connections. People like me, we work for every opportunity. We have nothing handed to us."

"What did you do?" Detective Price repeated.

"Tell them about the board," Tatiana ordered. "Tell them how *that man* was given special privileges the rest of us didn't know of."

I backed up two steps. I didn't like the look in her eye.

She rushed forward, her strong musician fingers catching my shoulders and digging in. "Tell them."

I tried to break loose, but her grip was too tight. So I did what she wanted. "The board wasn't going to make him reaudition when everyone else did."

The detectives probably heard my words—Jack, at least, was good at noticing everything—but they didn't give any sign that they had. Instead, Detective Lock's hand had gone to his gun. Detective Watson's hands had gone up as she stepped forward.

And Detective Price's face was turning a deep red. He took half a step forward.

Not sure what he had in mind, and worried about what Tatiana would do if Detective Price—Jack—startled her, I motioned for him to stay back.

His face continued to darken, but he held back.

Silence enveloped us. A tense silence, like the waiting of a leading tone hanging in the air unresolved.

Finally, Detective Price's deep voice settled the air. "Ms. King, would you like to explain how your DNA came to be under the victim's fingernails?"

One of Tatiana's hands drifted from my

shoulder to her head. "I don't know what you're talking about."

Instead of trying to get away now that she only had me by one shoulder, I took the cue of Irene's raised hands to try to placate Tatiana. "Everyone knows Ludwig was a little obsessed when it came to his job."

Tatiana nodded, her eyes wide. "He deserved to be hurt. He was going to stay here, without ever reauditioning, until he had a better position lined up. It wasn't fair, and I told him so. The man laughed at me for going to the board. Laughed! I told him he'd be sorry."

"What did he say?" If I could keep her talking, maybe she'd forget she was holding onto me.

She blinked. "He tried to knock me aside, but his hand caught in my hair. I pushed him. His nails dug into my scalp as he fell."

Detective Watson grabbed me, pulling me away from Tatiana's grasp as Detective Price's handcuffs found their place around the violinist's wrists.

Twenty-Six

My spot behind the speakers had been taken by cannons.

In the fluster of the day, I'd forgotten I'd need to claim a different place for the concert.

Not that they were using those cannons for the 1812 Overture—they were just for show. The cannons they'd be using were back by the administration buildings, where the sound wouldn't be quite so deafening for the audience.

The grass was filling up with blankets and chairs. I wandered through the crowd hoping to find a perfect spot until the sound of my name being called broke me out of my search.

I looked around.

"Octavia, over here!" Arms waving overhead, Cora caught my eye. She was sitting on a blanket, surrounded by her kids and a woman who looked so much like Cora that she had to be her mother.

I hurried over to give Cora a hug. "I'm so glad you could come."

"We couldn't miss it," she said, pulling away so she could ruffle the hair of the boy standing protectively beside her. "Not with the concert being dedicated to Ludwig. They chose his favorite music and everything."

"Everyone wanted to make sure he was remembered well," I said. It was true. Even though Ludwig had been obnoxious, he was still one of them.

After a few minutes of chatting, I excused myself. I still had to find a place to sit. Eventually, I decided to go up and watch the concert from the pond across from the shop. I wouldn't be able to see very well, and the music wouldn't be as loud, but it would be nice to be alone for a bit. It would give me a chance to detox from all the peopling.

The shop had been crazy busy all day, but I don't think we'd sold anything. All people wanted to do was talk. And all they wanted to talk about was Tatiana's arrest.

Piper was beside herself that she'd been backstage and had missed everything except watching Detective Solved-The-Case leading Tatiana away.

Xavier, of course, had gotten the details from me, then talked to everyone as if he'd been there himself. I was down with that, since it meant I didn't have to repeat things so often.

My friends had been hoping the detectives might stop by and fill in the details for us, but they never did.

Not that it mattered.

Except it did. They'd inserted themselves in our lives—my life—so much for a few days that it felt strange to not have them around.

I laughed. It was hard to believe I'd gotten used to having law enforcement people around, or that I missed them now the case was wrapped up and they were gone.

The music was distant enough that I decided to just go to the shop. I might as well take inventory so I could see if we needed to order anything.

As I was counting the strings, there was a knock on the door, making me lose count of how many E strings were in the pile. "We're closed," I yelled.

I pushed my glasses up the bridge of my nose and started counting over, but the knock came again.

"Octavia?"

Giving up, I tucked the strings back in their spot and headed for the door. Mairi could do inventory in the morning. She enjoyed it almost as much as she liked cleaning away fingerprints from the display cases.

Light spilled through the glass door, shining on Cora's face. I unlocked the door. "I thought you were at the concert."

She nodded. "It's intermission. I was going to say something before, but with the kids there I didn't want to bring it up. The insurance company is giving me a hard time. They want to make sure Ludwig's violin is safe after everything that's happened."

"Of course they do." They could have at least waited a few weeks out of respect for the family's grief.

She spoke quickly, as if afraid of my reaction. "The thing is, since it's not in police custody, they want pictures to prove it's still in one piece. Silly, I know."

"Okay, come in. You can get your pictures of the Gagliano and be back to the concert in time to hear the 1812."

I led her back to the office, spun the combination dial and opened the safe.

There, looking lonely all by itself, was Ludwig's case. I moved it over to the desk and undid the zipper and clasp, then lifted the lid.

The warm patina of the varnish seemed to glow, and the light caught the spot on the E string that was beginning to unravel.

No wonder Ludwig hadn't wanted to wait for the one he'd ordered. If he'd kept playing on that much longer it would have started to rattle when the string vibrated, not to mention it would be annoying to press that part of the string against the fingerboard, even with callused fingertips.

Cora pulled out her phone and started taking pictures. "Could you lift it so I can get a shot of the back?"

"Of course." As I lifted the instrument, I noticed the little envelope tucked under the scroll. Normally I wouldn't think anything of it, but Ludwig kept his spare strings in the string tube next to his bow. I could see three strings in it without even looking closely.

If my brain had been music, it would have jumped from moving at *adagio* to *presto* in the length of a breath.

Why would Ludwig have come to the shop and made a scene about the fact that we didn't have the string he wanted if he had one sitting in his case? Was it just to make a scene for the sake of making a scene?

Anyone else would be an automatic no, but this was Ludwig. He enjoyed making a scene.

But he said the one he'd ordered hadn't arrived before he had to leave for the mountain. Maybe it made me naïve, but I'd believed him.

"That should be enough," Cora said. She was looking through the pictures on her phone.

As I set the Gagliano back in the case, I took another look at the envelope. Definitely an E string.

Which meant something. Something big.

And just like that, I knew. "Cora, why would the insurance be asking for proof that the Gagliano is safe? They shouldn't be wanting pictures unless you were updating the appraisal or filing a claim for damage."

I know sometimes people thought I lived in my own version of reality instead of the real world, but I'd been a musician all my life. I knew how these things worked.

There was a click behind me. "Move away from the violin, Octavia."

I looked over my shoulder at the tone of Cora's voice.

The barrel of a gun looked back at me.

Twenty-Seven

I RAISED MY HANDS IN an all too familiar motion. "Cora, we're friends. Put the gun down."

If you've ever had a gun pointed at you, you know that no matter how many times it happens you'll always feel that fight or flight reflex kick in.

What, you've never had a gun pointed at you before? Well, I have, so take it from me. The other times I'd had a gun trained on me, it had been a cop holding it. Having my friend—okay, so we weren't *good* friends, but still—holding the gun made it worse.

"Move away from the Gagliano," Cora repeated.

I shook my head. Staying close to the violin was my best chance at not getting shot. I was sure Cora would rather sell the instrument than jump through all the hoops to get the insurance to pay out.

What? I've heard that kind of thing takes forever.

"Step away from the violin and slowly walk toward me." As she spoke, one of her hands left the butt of the gun and fished in her oversized purse.

I thought about rushing her, but her right hand seemed awfully steady, and call me crazy, but I didn't want to get shot.

Cora pulled a bundle of paracord from the purse and hung it over her shoulder. "Come on."

Being careful to keep the violin right behind me, I took a tiny step forward.

She motioned again.

The gun signaled to my brain that I should be cooperating. I've made it a practice to always go willingly when I'm arrested—it's easier on everyone—so it was hard to stand my ground, but I did it.

"I don't have time for this," Cora snapped. She tried to wave me closer again. "Intermission was ending when I got here. They're playing the 1812 right now, and I need to time the gunshot with the cannon fire so no one hears."

She was going to kill me with the beat. I bit back a laugh I was sure would have sounded hysterical. So much of the time in orchestral and chamber music, violists keep the beat, so maybe her plan for me was fitting.

But being a metronome was a part of playing the viola I'd never loved. What I loved was the rich tones, and harmonizing with melodies, and supporting the other musicians.

No. I wasn't going to let her decide how I was going out. I just needed to figure out how to defend myself from the crazy lady with bullets.

A comment Piper had made once upon a time

popped into my head, and I smiled. The best way to defend myself was to make Cora listen to all my thoughts.

"When you showed up and wanted to see the Gagliano, how did you know it was here? Detective Price didn't announce that to anyone. At first I thought he'd told you, but I've realized that if he had, he'd have told me so I knew it was okay."

"I don't have time to answer questions. You'll just have to die without the little villain speech. Come on." She gestured me forward.

I moved an inch toward her so it would look like I was cooperating. "Killing me is only going to make things worse when the detectives figure out you killed Ludwig."

She took a step toward me. "Stop trying to distract me."

I looked at the shrinking space between us. The office wasn't very big. It would take maybe two good-sized steps and she'd be able to reach me. "Can you back up? I don't like being this close to a gun."

Cora spluttered.

I kept talking, saying anything that popped into my head. I told Cora about Ludwig's deal with the board that he could stay with the symphony as long as he wanted. I told her Mairi would figure out what happened to me when she saw the E string in Ludwig's case. I told her all about my breakup with Morton.

The longer I went on, the glassier her eyes got, and her grip loosened on the gun.

When the first cannon finally fired, she startled as if the gun had accidentally gone off.

Knowing I wouldn't get another chance, I dove at Cora.

My momentum sent us careening into the side of the safe. The gun flew from Cora's hand.

We rolled on the floor, Cora trying to punch me, and me trying to avoid her fists, until she rolled off me and climbed to her feet. Her head moved like a bobblehead doll saying no as she looked around.

I saw the gun on the floor below the window at the same time she did. I grabbed her leg as she started to run toward it, pulling her back down.

Then it became a race. I didn't know what to do with a gun. What I knew was that I didn't want her to have it. But I was losing. All my energy was going to keeping her from getting ahead. There wasn't enough left in me to get in front of her.

When her shoe came off in my hand, I reacted as only someone who hates shoes would.

I smashed it into the back of Cora's head as hard as I could.

She fell.

All I wanted to do was fall on the ground beside her, but I had no idea how quickly she'd wake up.

Well, it's not as if I'd ever hit someone with a shoe before.

Or anything else, for that matter.

I grabbed the paracord and tied her wrists and ankles together. Then, for good measure, I tied her knees, too.

What now? Detective Price thought he already had Ludwig's killer in custody.

Panting, I fell into the desk chair and pushed my glasses into place as I looked around the office for something to tell me what to do. And there, mostly tucked under the computer, was the answer.

I pulled the card out and looked at it. Detective Jack Price, followed by two phone numbers. One was marked *cell.*

On the floor, Cora was moaning. I grabbed a polishing cloth off the desk and tied it around her mouth. Hopefully that would do the job.

Hating it, but knowing I didn't have any choice, I nudged the shop phone so I could see the numbers.

Deep breaths, Octavia. It probably won't kill you, but if Cora gets free, she will.

I tapped in the number to Detective Price's cell phone. Then I pushed the button I'd seen Mairi and Xavier use when they didn't want to have to hold the phone, and I stood as far away as I could.

Ringing came out of the speaker, then a deep voice spoke. "Price."

"Jack," I yelled at the phone, hoping it would pick up my voice even though I wasn't right next to it.

"Octavia? What's wrong?" His voice was quieter than I wanted, and I had to move closer to hear.

"Tatiana didn't kill Ludwig."

"Why are you yelling at me?" he asked. He didn't wait for an answer. "I know it wasn't Tatiana. It was the ex-wife. When we were questioning Tatiana, the woman said Ludwig was alive when she left. She said she could prove it. All we had to do was ask the ex-wife who passed her in the doorway."

I know it was silly, considering what I'd just been through, but I was annoyed he already knew. Let's pretend that it was because I felt he could have stopped Cora coming after me and not because I wanted to be the one to have solved the case.

"I've already been to her house," Jack was saying, "but she isn't there. One of the neighbors said there was a concert in Ludwig's memory tonight and the family had gone there."

I nodded. Oh, right, he couldn't see me.

"If you see her, stay away from her. She could be dangerous."

Could be dangerous? *Could be?* There was no *could* be about it. And she was maybe just the teensiest bit crazy.

"That might be hard. Staying away from her, I mean."

"Why would it be hard?"

I glanced over to Cora. She was twisting her wrists, testing the knots, and glaring at me. "Because I have her tied up on my office floor."

Jack cursed like only a cop or a sailor could, and I thought I heard an engine revving in the background. "I'll be right there."

Twenty-Seven

A FEW DAYS LATER, WE were just closing the shop when Jack walked in.

Xavier made yummy noises under his breath.

I had to agree, the detective cleaned up nice—but the cleaned-up detective didn't have anything on Jack when his sandy hair was rumpled.

Not that I'd ever get to see that again.

"Hi," Jack said. His hands were in his pockets, making him look more at ease than I'd ever seen him.

"Hey." I straightened my glasses. After giving my statement a thousand times, or at least half a dozen, I hadn't seen any of the detectives. I'd started to think they were going to just slip away without saying goodbye.

He gave me his Detective Devastating smile. "Do you have time for a walk?"

"Sure." I glanced at my employees. Mairi was pretending not to pay attention, but Xavier made puppy eyes at the idea of missing out on any gossip

Jack might share. "Once you've closed out, go ahead and go home. I'll see you tomorrow."

I breathed in deeply as I stepped through the door Jack held open for me. I'd never get enough of the fresh mountain air. "Where did you want to walk?"

"Wherever you like."

Well, if he didn't have anything in mind, we could walk around the little lake. There wasn't a bridge where the water left the pond and went down a short waterfall to run along the cliffside and behind the restaurant, but if I could hop across it, Jack's long legs certainly could, too.

We walked halfway around the pond in silence. You might think that would be awkward, walking along with a detective, but it wasn't. Then Jack stopped and leaned against a boulder. "Cora says she didn't mean to kill him."

"Do you believe her?" I pushed myself up to sit on the rock.

He shrugged. "Her intent isn't for me to decide, but no. I don't think it was premeditated, but she was really angry with him. I think, in that moment, she would have done anything to put an end to the guy."

I thought for a minute. "Why was she mad at him?"

"Did you know she used to play the violin?"

I shook my head. I'd known Ludwig and Cora for several years, and this was the first I was hearing of it.

Maybe she'd been asking about the Gagliano because she wanted to claim it for herself.

Jack looked out across the view below. Tiny people moved around the amphitheater, probably getting it ready for the next concert. "To hear Cora tell it, she was a better musician than Ludwig. She put her violin away when they had kids and didn't look back until the man left her. Now she misses it, but she said something about rusty fingers."

"It's easy to lose finger dexterity. We joke that it feels like your joints have rusted." I didn't play as often as I should, but I'd managed to avoid that so far. Hopefully I'd always keep the rust at bay. I didn't like the idea of my fingers tightening up on me. "Ludwig made her stop playing?"

"She says someone had to take care of the kids. She was happy to do it, at first. But after the divorce she realized Ludwig had manipulated her into being the one to quit. At least, she's convinced he did." He hesitated, and I knew we were getting to the real reason Ludwig had died. "She sacrificed for those kids. I'm sure he did, too. That's what being a parent is. But he was trying to take the kids away from her. When she brought him that string she told him she planned to fight for them."

"And Ludwig didn't like being told he couldn't have his way." I'd never seen him take that kind of loss gracefully. Musicians are an emotional bunch. We have to tap into all those feelings to make the notes come alive, and that can't happen if we bury them. But Ludwig's emotions lived on the surface without any control. "So she got mad and hit him."

"She did." He looked at me then, and I saw a deep sadness in his eyes that I didn't know how to chase away.

I wasn't even sure I should try. Instead of poking in where I didn't know I'd be welcome, I asked about Cora. "What comes next?"

"She's been charged with murder, along with attempted murder for what she did to you. She's admitted to sending you the threat in the mail, and for causing the trouble at your home." He took a breath before continuing. "Apparently you met with her when you went to visit your grandmother, and you and Detective Watson both forgot to mention it."

"I thought you knew."

He shook his head.

Oops. "When we left she was hurrying home to her kids."

"That might be what she wanted you to think, but she came up here instead." He looked like there was more he wanted to say about all that.

A part of me was mad at Cora for trying to scare me. Well, for everything she'd done. But the anger wouldn't help anyone. It was better to let it go. "What's going to happen to the kids?"

"Cora's mother has them. She's asked for guardianship, and I don't see any reason why she shouldn't get it."

We were quiet again, and I settled in deeper, listening to the water.

"You called me." His sudden statement pulled me back from the brink of meditation to see him watching me. "You don't use the phone, but you called me."

"Oh. That." It hadn't been as bad as I expected, but I wasn't going to admit it. Besides, I was blaming the less-than-horrifying experience on the fact that I was already freaked out about the whole being held at gunpoint by someone I thought was a friend thing. "Someone had to take care of Cora. I'm pretty good with knots, but I've never tied up a person before. She might have gotten free."

Those eyes that didn't miss anything saw right through me, but Jack was kind enough to keep any comments to himself. "Thank you for trusting me to come for you."

My belly was doing weird things again. "It's what friends do."

A strange look crossed his face.

Did that mean we weren't friends? Or that he thought we shouldn't be because I had a record and he gave people records? Or did he not like me? I mean, I know my vibe didn't resonate with everyone, but I couldn't help feeling a little bummed out.

His pocket buzzed at him. He fished his phone out of it and glanced at the screen. "It's about one of my other cases. I'm going to have to go."

Ouch. Rejected for work. Hopefully I hadn't actually flinched. "Okay."

Jack moved to stand in front of me. "What's next for you, Octavia? Are you heading back out on the road?"

I laughed. I rarely knew what was next in my life. "I'm here for the summer. After that, who knows?"

"Any protests coming up?"

"Always. There's one next weekend I was planning on going to."

"Try not to get arrested." He leaned forward, his hands bracketing my hips. "It would help if you didn't obstruct traffic, or block the sidewalks, or try to keep people out of government buildings. Make sure the organizers have a permit if they need one."

"You've been reading up on my arrests again." I bit my lip but couldn't hold back the smile.

"Don't let it go to your head." Jack chuckled, and my toes curled at the sound. Hopefully he didn't notice.

The man looked at reports and dealt with arrests all day, when he wasn't trying to solve murders. The fact that he'd looked at, let alone remembered the details about my arrests—well, of course that was going right to my head.

In Detective Holds-Himself-Back speak, it meant I was right. We were friends.

Jack chose that moment to lean in and brush his lips against mine.

All those emotions musicians swim in rose around me, and I melted.

He pulled away before I could get too drawn in. "Stay safe."

I stayed where I was until Piper came to find me.

"Xavier said Jack was here." She looked around at the obviously empty space around me. "Don't tell me you chased him off already."

I just smiled. I had a feeling I'd be seeing him again. Maybe I should get myself arrested and ask the arresting officer to call him in.

"Well, since you're not busy with the detective, come with me. I got my hands on a brand new trio I want to try, and I need a violist." Not bothering to wait for an answer, she pulled me off the rock and back around the pond, telling the story of how she'd convinced the composer to let her be the first to try his masterpiece.

"Who else is doing the read through?" I asked.

Her words came out as a mumble.

"Tell me you didn't say what I think you just said."

Piper took a deep breath, then tried again. "Tatiana."

That's what I thought I'd heard. I paused. On the inside, I was already walking away from the invitation. Then I thought about everything that had happened since Aerie Pines opened for the summer, and sitting at the music stand next to hers didn't seem so bad. "Okay."

"What?" Piper reached over and put the back of her hand against my forehead. "Are you okay?"

I grinned as I hurried toward the shop to get my viola.

Tatiana and I might never be close, but I had a feeling we could get along. After all, I was friends with a cop. Detective. Law enforcement person. Thing.

If that could happen, anything could.

Also by

Rebecca McKinnon

Clear Creek Mysteries
The Yarn That Binds
A Hill to Dye on
Purls Before Swine
Joy to the Wool

Standalone Novels
Beyond the Swearing Stone
Ankou's Daughter
Pockets of Deception

The Refuge Trilogy
Tenth Anniversary Collection
Annexed
Cantrip
Refuge

Pick the Plot Podcast Stories

In the Shadow of Scandal

Griselda's Revenge

Pirate's Blade

Crimson

Recipes Are Merely Suggestions

About the Author

Rebecca McKinnon enjoys playing with her imaginary friends and introducing them to others through her writing. She dreams of living in the middle of nowhere, but has been unable to find an acceptable location that wouldn't require crossing an ocean.

For more information about her, to learn more about her books, sign up for her newsletter, or contact her, please visit her website.

www.rebeccamckinnon.com